School's Out For Murder
An Alton Oaks Mystery

by

Megan Rivers

For information, email Cozy Cat Press, cozycatpress@aol.com or visit our website at: www.cozycatpress.com

COZY CAT
PRESS

ISBN: 978-1-946063-45-8
Printed in the United States of America

Cover design by Paula Ellenberger
www.paulaellenberger.com

10 9 8 7 6 5 4 3 2 1

To all the teachers who strive each day to put the students before a test score.

Thank you Leah, Brooke, the D.U. team, Ms. Baumer, Ms. Schmidt, and Miss Harrison

PROLOGUE

Alton Oaks, Illinois, was established in 1914, by my great-great-grandfather, Andrew Alton, when he was only thirty-two years old. He spent a great deal of his life as a U.S. Marshall. Not much is known before his time in service except that he was born in Missouri as Andrew Alexander Alton on September 7, 1882.

He started his career as a U.S. Marshall when he was just seventeen and continued to travel the country in the early twentieth century, tracking outlaws and bringing thieves and murderers to justice. Some notable captures included "Mad" Jonas Brown, Thomas "Tall T" Zigler, and Johnny "Joe John" Johnson.

Andrew Alton met my great-great-grandmother, Agnes, a Norwegian immigrant, when he was thirty years old—in 1912—while they were both on a train headed to Moline via Chicago and married soon after.

After unsuccessfully catching notorious bank thief D. B. Williams, the trail ended in what is now Alton Oaks. Some town legends say that Andrew found a clue here which prevented him from leaving; others say he simply gave up and retired to properly raise a family. We may never know the real reason of whatever happened to D. B. Williams.

Many people don't know that when early settlers moved west, they cut down many of the oak trees for lumber to build homes. The oak trees Andrew Alton came across were only about one hundred years old and were probably acorns or saplings at the time the early settlers drove by on their covered wagons.

Andrew Alton bought the land, which stretched from what is now Sheridan to Terryville. The purchase was a total of 35.57 square miles, of which 18.16 miles was shoreline along the Whett River. Andrew Alton was able to purchase this with the reward money he collected as a U.S. Marshall. Not long after, he began selling the timber and made a small fortune over the next five years. He eventually sold the land that became Sheridan and Terryville—along with its valuable shoreline, adding to his personal worth.

During this time, his new wife Agnes gave birth to two sons, Anders and Gregor, after a heartbreaking stillborn in the winter of 1915 that nearly killed Agnes with grief.

To keep his mind off the devastating news of the stillborn, Andrew drew up plans for the Alton House— a historical building that still stands today—and supervised the building between the spring of 1915 and the winter of 1916. Town records report that Andrew and Agnes lived in a small cabin while the house was being built on land where Gnarled Circle Drive is located today. The couple were able to move in with their newest addition to the family—oldest living son, Anders Alton.

The house looks slightly different today than what Andrew Alton built: In the 1940s, a second floor was added when a fire destroyed the south side of the building, making the kitchen and back porch slightly, more up-to-date—by 1940's standards.

Tragically, my great-great-grandfather didn't get to see his two sons grow up. On the morning of July 5, 1920, Andrew Alton was found dead on the steps of town hall—murdered. And while his son Anders grew old with a family of his own—he was my great-grandfather—he was only four years old when he lost his father. To this day, no one has solved the mystery of who murdered our town's founder.

Regardless of the tragedies found in our past, we can still celebrate the milestones our ancestors reached for us to be here today. Whether your distant family traveled to a new home in a new country or farmed for countless generations, the important thing to remember is that they lived. They did the best with what they had and not one of us would be standing here today without their hardships.

CHAPTER ONE

"Thanks again for coming in so early," Principal Lisah Newton said as she opened the gym doors and the ripe smell of middle school children clung to the air. She wore a starkly white blouse beneath her starchy dark blue pantsuit and her unnaturally blonde hair was kept tight in a French twist on her head. Despite the muggy day we were having, not one hair was out of place nor a lick of perspiration found glistening in the corners of her skin.

"Oh, it's no problem. I'm glad I can help out. I'm glad Jenna thought to recommend me," I admitted, following her into the gym. We walked across the basketball court to the door at the far end of the hall, where I assumed more classrooms were.

My cousin (and neighbor), Jenna, is the Exceptional Students Coordinator throughout Alton Oaks, Terryville, and Sheridan, which means she works with both gifted and special needs students in all the schools and manages their services. She heard me moaning about not having a job and as I had a background as an ELL teacher, she thought I'd be perfect for the elementary school's summer learning program. Presently, I was being taken on a tour of the school, though not much had changed since I was a student here in the nineties.

Principal Newton's heeled shoes *clack-clacked* over the wooden floor, echoing throughout the quiet space. It was still too early for school to begin, but some kids were already starting to gather on the playground behind the building. "Oh, we love Mrs. Silva," the principal gushed as she held open the door that led out of the gymnasium. "The amount of growth her students show each year is astounding."

The wide metal gym door poured into another hallway with four doors. Principal Newton propped it open, flipping the door jamb down with the toe of her black patent leather heel and then nodded her head, gesturing to the door across the hall. "Here is the supply closet on the north end of the school, in case you need paper or pencils," she shared and led me further down the hallway.

There was little more than a week left of school and the bulletin boards in the hallways were bare and most classrooms were packed up and bland in color. They reminded me of hospital rooms.

As we approached the last door at the end of the hallway, I automatically noticed the long, thin window above the door knob. It was still covered in a colorful collage of children's artwork. The principal let her hand rest on the knob for a moment and said, "This is Ms. Dempsey's fifth grade room. This will be the room you will be using this summer." She knocked and waited for a response, but none came. "She's usually here early, but I guess not today."

I was disappointed that Ms. Dempsey wasn't in because I had heard such great things about her from our gossipy town. Nevertheless, Principal Newton opened the door to show me the classroom I'd be using.

It wasn't the bright colors, the yoga balls as chairs, the life-size completed skeleton, or the tactile tools and manipulatives any teacher would die to have in their classroom that I noticed first. No.

It was the body hanging from the ceiling beside the teacher's desk.

In a knee-length black skirt and a blouse adorned

with rose buds, Ms. Dempsey hovered over the multi-colored, block-patterned rug. Her shoulder-length, dark-blonde hair revealed a face that was no longer beautiful, but swollen with burst capillaries. In horrific shock, I ran back into the hallway to violently deposit my breakfast into the closest garbage can as the ghastly scene burned onto the back of my eyelids, haunting me.

Principal Newton gripped the door with one hand and covered her mouth with the other as she slowly closed the door in disbelief. It was probably the first time in her life she experienced such a shock. She struck me as the person who planned everything and lived by routine and color-coordinated outlines.

Hunched over on my knees and with one arm gripping the garbage can, I pulled my cell phone from my pocket and dialed Jake's number, the Alton Oaks deputy who'd put the last town murderer behind bars.

"Jake Vega," he answered.

"Jake, it's Charli," I said, my throat sore from vomiting. "You need to get down to the elementary school right away."

Whether it was the tone of my voice, or my affinity for being in the wrong place at the wrong time, Jake didn't need any more details. "On my way," he said and hung up the phone.

Alton Oaks wasn't large and the school was three streets from the police station, so when Jake entered the gym before I found the strength to stand up, I wasn't surprised. His face was flushed and sweat from the humid morning collected above his lip and I assumed he either ran or rode a police bicycle over.

"I don't get it," Principal Newton said, regaining her senses. "She was getting *married*." She sighed, her tone getting rough and agitated. "Now I'll have to cancel school and find a substitute to finish out the year."

Jake surveyed the hallway and, finding no reason for

alarm, extended an arm to help me from the floor. I shook my head, knitting my eyebrows together. "In there, Jake." I pointed to the door behind Principal Newton.

As the principal muttered to herself, she pulled out her cell phone and began getting to work. "Excuse me, I have to tend to these matters," she spat angrily and her heels *clack-clacked* across the gymnasium floor, growing fainter as Jake approached the classroom door.

After shooting me a look of confusion, he put his hand on the door knob; the other lightly touched the gun that rested in the holster on his hip. As he opened the door to the rising sun in the distant windows, the deathly shadow of Ms. Dempsey's demise traveled down the hallway. The long silhouette of her stiff legs ended inches from where I sat, and another wave of nausea was about to pummel my insides.

CHAPTER TWO

"Seriously, Charli?" my best friend Sadie asked, plopping down on the other end of the two-seater booth I occupied at The Buzz Coffee shop on Main Street. "How is it you always find yourself in the middle of these juicy situations?"

Sadie wasn't at all worried about my physical safety. She was exasperated at how "lucky" I had been lately when I found myself smack-dab in the middle of the town's hottest gossip—especially when it came so close to some of the unusual deaths taking place in our hometown recently. It's true that this past spring, only two short months ago, my nosiness helped out the police department and put a murderer behind bars, but it also gave me a stab in the back—literally—with a pair of sewing sheers. My left shoulder was still tender from the nearly healed wound.

Both of my hands wrapped around the large, deep maroon coffee mug and I wished it was something stronger. Getting stabbed was physically worse than what I'd experienced that morning, but the image of Ms. Dempsey, in her nylons and shoeless feet, hovering in the air, would haunt my dreams for the rest of my life. I closed my eyes and took a deep breath of roasted coffee beans, vanilla, and caramel, thankful that the nausea had passed before I left the school.

"Sorry, Charli," Sadie said regretfully after realizing I wasn't over it. "Are you okay?"

Taking a sip of the strongest coffee the shop offered, I nodded. "I will be." The mug had made the stainless steel spoon on the table tinkle when I set it back down. "It was horrible, Sadie; she was just hanging there."

Sadie offered a sympathetic look. Her auburn hair danced over her shoulders as she discreetly looked at the patrons in the coffee shop who were not being at all tactful in the way they were eavesdropping on our conversation. The Buzz was always the place to find the newest and hottest gossip in Alton Oaks... other than my mother's front porch.

"Come on," Sadie said, bouncing up from her seat. "Let's go for a walk."

Leaving my half-empty mug behind, I let her lead me back into the sunshine. "Exercise and fresh air will make you feel better, and ice cream!" Sadie exclaimed, leading me next door to Froz T's walk-up window. Though the store had just opened for the day, there was already a growing line at the walk-up window. *It's going to be a hot, muggy day*, I thought as I wiped the perspiration from my forehead. I could already feel the angry morning sun burning my scalp.

After receiving our traditional ice cream tacos— Sadie even sprung for brownie bites and rainbow sprinkles—we walked down Main Street, towards the river, in hopes of catching a stray breeze. "Does Jake know anything about what happened?" Sadie asked.

The sugar was definitely helping me find normalcy again. In between licking the ice cream that oozed down my wrist, I answered, "No. He called in the chief and then they called the crime scene unit that came in for Sara's murder in April. I left after they took my statement." Church bells rang in the distance as I added, "I didn't want to stay."

"Yikes. I can't believe it. First a murder and now a suicide. Alton Oaks is changing," she mused as we crossed the intersection of Main and Oak. "I've heard nothing but good things about Ms. Dempsey from the kids," Sadie shared. She was a pediatric nurse at St. Collette's Hospital on the west side of town.

"Oh Sadie," I said, widening my eyes with awe. "You would not believe her classroom." I tried to shrug away the image of her stiff, swaying body with a fierce shiver that wiggled my shoulders despite the heat rising off the pavement. "All the other rooms were bland and packed up for the summer, but hers was still in full swing. She had stability balls instead of chairs for the kids, personal sandboxes for the kids to use instead of paper for spelling and math, a butterfly cocoon near the window, and *so many* books. She must have been a wonderful teacher to be able to reach so many levels and abilities in her room."

"Sounds like I wanna go back to fourth grade," Sadie shared and then popped the last bite of her ice cream taco into her mouth.

"Fifth grade," I corrected.

She shrugged at my comment and licked her fingers with indifference.

We passed a few stores in silence as the reality of what had hit our town began to sink in, making us both feel vulnerable.

When we could see the glistening river just behind Town Circle up ahead, I asked, "Did you know she was getting married?"

Sadie shook her head, moving her gaze from the boats that traveled down the river to me and answered, "I didn't know the woman personally. Just her reputation as a teacher."

As we walked past the steps of town hall, Sadie interjected, "That's weird though."

"What is?" I asked, kicking some wood chips back into the flower bed as we passed.

"Most women dream about their wedding their whole life, you know?" The question brought me back to the time when Sadie and I watched *The Sound of Music* when we were nine and I vowed to have a wedding just like Georg and Maria, with the long white train, organ music, and an angelic choir in the background. Sadie laughed in my face at the time and told me hers would be at the zoo in Chicago and full of hot pink leopard print. Smiling with nostalgia, I nodded in agreement.

"Someone who is about to get married wouldn't be a good candidate for suicide," Sadie pointed out as we reached the Whett River Canal Trail path.

Letting the breeze erase our perspiration as we walked east, I answered, "Maybe they had a fight or he couldn't commit to a date, or he called it off." Without skipping a beat, I added, "Or maybe he cheated on her and she couldn't take it."

Sadie tugged on my arm to show support. My husband had cheated on me, but I didn't end my life. No, I drastically packed a suitcase, hailed a cab, and came to Alton Oaks. Two months ago. And I haven't gone back.

"Have you heard from him?" Sadie asked, referring to Jackson, my husband.

I shrugged. It didn't get any easier to talk about what had happened, but at least the wound wasn't as fresh and tender. "He calls."

"What does he say?" she asked and threw the container that held her ice cream taco away in a green metal trash can along the canal.

Again, I shrugged. I fished my cell phone out from the back pocket of my shorts and handed it to her. "I haven't answered."

"Bottomless Butt Fries, Charli!" Sadie exclaimed with one of her trademark G-rated profanities. "One hundred and eight text messages? Twenty-eight voicemails? Are all of these from him?!"

I lifted and dropped my shoulders once more, not wanting to sacrifice any words to this conversation.

"Doesn't that flashing blue light and mail icon bother you?" Sadie asked thumbing through screens.

Yeah, they did. It was like Jackson was constantly poking me in the ribs when that blue light flashed in the middle of the night, reminding me of the unanswered messages. It'd be nice to get rid of them, but then I'd have to deal with Jackson, however distantly.

Sadie must have sensed the internal struggle and hesitantly offered, "Do you want me to weed through them and see if there's anything important? That way you don't really have to deal with it?"

I should have said no, put on my big girl panties, and done it myself, but I was still so broken on the inside. I just couldn't. Biting my bottom lip with anxiety, I nodded slightly.

With a reassuring smile, Sadie bent her head over the phone, determined to help me deal with this burden. Once in awhile Sadie would sigh, let out a disgruntled "Ha!" or mutter one of her creatively colorful swear words under her breath. At one point she couldn't keep it in and reported, "Wow. What a class act. He wrote 'Stop overreacting and come home so we can work through this,' using each letter in separate text messages. How did he think that was going to solve anything?"

Apprehensively, I played with the hair that fell over my shoulder, despite it being in a ponytail, until Sadie finally said, "There's nothing important in the text messages but guilt trips, anger, and manipulation. I am deleting them for your own good." I didn't argue with her.

We reached the path that cut through the oak trees that connected the canal path to the residents on Gnarled Circle Drive, the high-end subdivision where

Sadie grew up and veered to it. Sadie had the cell phone to her right ear and her left hand covered her left ear in order to hear the messages more clearly.

When we reached the large patch of oak trees between Gnarled Circle Drive and the Alton house, Sadie put down the phone and hesitated. "Well," she began, "a lot of the calls at the beginning were a plea for forgiveness, then ultimatums, and then anger. Then there were a few with questions like how to pay for the electricity because the power went out, and the passcode for the joint bank account. And then," she swallowed hard, not wanting to divulge the last piece of information, "he was evicted for not paying rent. He said if you wanted anything you'd left behind, you'd have to pay the building manager what was owed. Otherwise it would be auctioned off for the debt."

Sitting down on a fallen tree trunk, I buried my face in my hands. Sadie joined me, her added weight to the trunk made it shift slightly and creak. Placing her hand on my shoulder, she asked, "Can I do anything?"

Several moments passed as I let this information sink in. "Ya know," I said, dropping my hands from my face, "it's kind of a good thing. I mean, I took all the really important stuff with me." I paused with stark realization. "There's no reason to go back now. Really, there isn't. Okay, so I won't have my iPod dock, or printer, or that one painting I bought from the artist on the corner, but that's fine. Sure, my credit score probably plummeted, but I have everything I need, everything that's important to me is here." I looked over at Sadie who wore a mask of surprise. "Really," I said and I meant it.

Was this a hint of the healing I so desperately beckoned? Did this realization mean I was on the road to recovery and possible forgiveness? Things would get easier from here, right?

Sadie put her arms around me for a hug. "You're either the strongest person I know, or you're going to have one heck of a breakdown," she commented.

CHAPTER THREE

The following evening was the elementary school's Heritage Fair. Principal Newton did not hesitate to reopen the school and reassured the community that the horrific events that had happened on campus would in no way affect the success of this event. I doubted the psychological effects of Ms. Dempsey's fifth grade class being held by a substitute teacher, in another classroom, so soon after losing their beloved teacher, ever crossed her mind.

Weeks ago I had been asked to speak at the Heritage Fair regarding the history of the town since my great-great-grandfather was the one who founded it. Jenna and my mother urged me to take on the project, so my spring had been filled with taking trips to the library to research the facts, dates, numbers, and names of my ancestry. And I prepared a sweet PowerPoint: evidence of my lack of a life.

On Thursday night, Mom and I arrived at the elementary school together. Since she was the children's activity coordinator at the library, she was setting up a station about heritage using a variety of library resources and books.

The gym held tables of display boards made by the students and the smell of free coffee hung in the air as the young children of parent volunteers began chasing each other in the empty space of the gymnasium, sending echoes of pounding feet and shrieks of joy bouncing off the high ceiling. Several times my eyes glanced over at the door that led to the hallway where

Ms. Dempsey's classroom was, as I set up my computer on the small platform stage. It was the same stage that I once toppled over the edge of in second grade, dressed as a Native American for a Thanksgiving pageant.

The janitor, dressed in his trademark uniform of blue jeans and a long-sleeve white t-shirt, bounced silently around the gym. His silhouette moved like a ghost, unnoticed and blending into the background. He connected wires from the microphone to the speakers, set up extra tables for the PTA, and took away the already full garbage liner by the kitchen, where parents were drinking their weight in coffee and buying pastries to fund next year's football uniforms. At one point, I caught his eye while he unfolded an extra chair on the stage and I gave him a friendly wave. He dismissed it, looked down, and disappeared into the growing crowd. I made a mental note to introduce myself to him the next time I saw him in the hallways during the day.

Slowly, families began shuffling in from the warm night air until the gym seemed packed to capacity. Exactly at seven o'clock, Principal Newton's black matte pumps *clack-clacked* across the wooden stage to the podium as I nervously sat on a chair to the side, every so often reminding myself to stop biting my nails.

A crackle and short, curt feedback squeal from the microphone brought the volume of voices in the room down considerably as they all turned toward the platform stage.

"Welcome to Heritage Night," Principal Newton began, her hair not moving from its French twist as she looked from her notes on the podium to the faces in the crowd.

"Thank you for finding the time to support your community and your child's learning tonight, despite the recent unfortunate events that played out on our campus this week. Ms. Dempsey was a teacher who will be missed and rest-assured that we are working with a team of available grief counselors in order to help our students adjust to this shock, despite the limited number of days left in this school year." Principal Newton paused for a moment, and I swear I could see her lips silently count to five, just to be sure she gave enough time before switching topics.

"Heritage Night is a long-standing tradition of River Oaks Elementary, beginning in 1973. It is a chance for our students to practice comprehension in several informational text standards by researching, analyzing resources, explaining relationships in historical texts, and sometimes even analyzing multiple accounts of the same event or person from our town's history. During our Historical Heritage studies, students even sharpen their writing, presentation, speaking, and listening skills, which are important parts of the Common Core curriculum." As Principal Newton began talking about curriculum and standards, my mind started to drift back to my class of ELL students. I'd left them behind without a goodbye in New Mexico when I suddenly moved back to Illinois in April. My heart was heavy for them, and I still felt guilty for leaving without an explanation. God, I missed them.

Principal Newton cleared her throat, bringing my attention back to my current reality in Alton Oaks. "Before we begin, we are lucky enough to have the great-great-granddaughter of Andrew Alton to speak to us about her heritage, which is important to all of Alton Oaks' residents. Please give a warm welcome to Ms. Charlotte Parker who has donated a lot of her free time to bring this presentation to you tonight." Principal Newton stepped aside and raised a hand, motioning for me to join her. I only hoped I wouldn't relive my second grade stumble as I walked across the platform in my mother's fancy wedges.

"Hello," I said nervously and stopped to clear my throat when a small squeal of feedback from the microphone greeted me. Taking a deep breath, my gaze swept across the crowd. More faces looked familiar now than when I moved back to Alton Oaks only two months ago. A smile crept across my face when I saw Sadie and my brother, Alex, standing beside Jake: some of my favorite Alton Oaks residents. Pulling confidence from their encouraging gazes, I looked down at my notes and began sharing what I'd learned about my family and their historic role in this town.

When I ran out of PowerPoint slides and ended with the unsolved mystery of my great-great-grandfather's murder, the dose of adrenaline coursing through me had me feeling a bit disappointed that my presentation was over. "Are there any questions?" I heard myself asking, even though it wasn't planned.

A number of hands shot into the air and I was pleased, as any teacher would be, that I'd captivated the audience and instilled in them a desire to know more. "How did he die?" a blonde-haired kid with a bowl cut asked. He wore a baseball jersey and couldn't have been more than ten years old.

"He was murdered, found on the steps of Town Hall early in the morning of July 5, 1920. Medical records report that he was shot in the chest at close range." I wanted to add that the shot didn't cause him to die immediately, but incapacitated him; he died from a loss of blood, looking up at the sky, helpless, from his place on the stairs. However, I thought it was too gruesome and inappropriate considering the fresh horrors of Ms. Dempsey's fate and having so many young, impressionable minds in the audience.

"What happened to his wife and kids? What were their names again?" A junior high girl—probably the older sibling of one of the students—asked as she stood a few feet from a group of similarly aged youths, who were not paying attention to my speech.

"His wife, Agnes, remarried a timber man named Theodore Waight who went through most of Andrew's fortune. Andrew's oldest son, Anders, stayed in Alton Oaks and followed a political career, becoming the town mayor for the majority of his adult life. He got married and had a family. The younger brother, Gregor, went into law enforcement like his father. He died at the age of twenty-one in Chicago, during the famous shoot out with American gangster John Dillinger in 1934." The amount of death that seemed to creep into our lives suddenly struck me. Maybe Alton Oaks was never the wholesome hometown I thought it was.

"Wait; why is your last name Parker if your great-great-grandpa was named Alton, and this town's named Alton?" The pudgy boy who blurted out this question had a smug look on his face as he crossed his hands over his chest—like he caught the teacher in a lie, or worse: the wrong answer.

"Well," I began, taking a calming breath and putting on a smile. "My grandpa, Phillip Alton, had two kids: Randolph Alton—who is my uncle and the town's mayor," I paused and waved a hand towards my uncle who was near the free coffee and he waved. Then I continued, "and a daughter named Rose Alton, my mother. My mom married my father, Jeremy Parker—who is originally from Sheridan—and took his name. My mom was the first female Alton born in this country that we know of—the first female Alton born in over one hundred years. My uncle Randy had twin girls, so my brother, Alex, is the only male Alton heir, despite his last name being Parker." The know-it-all kid grew red in the face and dropped his arms from across his chest and melted back into the crowd.

A middle aged man in a John Deere hat and Carhartt

overalls then asked, "So no one's solved his murder case?" I assumed he was the father to one of the children behind a presentation board at a table nearby.

"Sadly, no," I replied. "The mystery of who killed Andrew Alton has remained unsolved to this day. It happened so long ago that I regret to admit that it might never be solved."

A hush fell upon the crowd—I would like to think it was out of respect for Andrew Alton, but in reality it was probably the lack of follow-up questions and the shortening length of attention spans.

Clack-clack went Principal Newton's heels as she closed the gap between her and the podium. "Thank you, Ms. Parker," she said, edging in between the microphone and me. "I would like to thank the Parker and Alton families for their time and for their part in keeping history alive in our town." There was a short applause and the murmuring began to rise in decibels until Principal Newton's voice grew in sternness. "I do have a few announcements before we conclude with the presentation. I would like to remind you that baked goods and refreshments are on sale at the cafeteria window to help the PTA fundraise for next year's budget and there is a sign-up list for parent volunteers regarding the Fall Program. Now, please enjoy the displays that the students created about their research into their own heritage."

As Principal Newton wrapped up, the crowd of parents, families, and students hesitated before turning to the displays. When the principal's shoes *clack-clacked* off the stage, it signaled the volume to ascend.

I stood at the podium to collect my notes, but got lost as I watched the crowd mull and adults mosey from table to table, from one glitter-encrusted display to another neon-papered presentation board.

The scene comforted me. Maybe it was because I

missed my class in Albuquerque, but I suddenly felt at home. Why did I stay away from Alton Oaks for so long? Sighing, I began dismantling the cords from my laptop as I pondered that question.

"Nice job," Jake said from below the podium. He was in off-duty clothes and I never got used to seeing him without his uniform these days. It seemed like he was always on duty. "I didn't know Andrew Alton was murdered, or maybe I just didn't remember," he shared, sliding his hands into the front pockets of his khakis.

Slipping my laptop back into its case, I added, "Yeah, it wasn't in the local history lessons in school. I think I found out about it in high school or junior high. I just remember doing a family tree project and Uncle Randy told me."

"There seems to be too much death here lately," Jake admitted almost defeatedly.

Any verbal reply seemed to give the truth power, so I only nodded my head, silently agreeing as I placed the last of my notes in the bag with my laptop.

"You did a fantastic job!" Sadie said from the floor in front of the stage. Although the platform was only two feet off the ground, Sadie's small stature made me feel like a giant.

I immediately jumped down from the platform to give her a hug. "Thanks, Sadie. I was super nervous," I admitted as Jake slipped back into the crowd behind her.

"You couldn't even tell!" Sadie reported with a hint of sarcasm around the edges.

Alex came up along side of her in a pair of starched jeans and a button-down brown and white short sleeved shirt that fit him as well as his white doctor's coat. "Great job, Charli May," he said, pulling me into a hug, which ultimately ended in a half-hearted noogie. His smile was radiant; it had always been a treat for me to get a compliment from my big brother.

"Thanks, Alex," I said, running a hand over my hair to fix the mess Alex made.

I want to say that it was weird seeing my life-long best friend and brother holding hands, but it wasn't. When I came back to Alton Oaks I found out that Alex and Sadie had been dating for several months. Anger never factored into my emotions; they were my two favorite people and they were incandescently happy together. It was only too natural to see them together now; I couldn't picture them ever coming apart. "Thanks for coming guys," I said, relieved the presentation was over and slung the laptop case over my good shoulder..

"Come on," Alex said with a wave. "I'll treat you both to one of Aunt Muriel's Sugar Shop Kitchen cupcakes," he offered, moving towards the cafeteria window. "If there are any left!" he added.

CHAPTER FOUR

Not long after the well of free coffee ran dry, families began to disappear from the gymnasium. An hour after my presentation began, I found myself helping my mother dismantle her display.

"Need some help, Mrs. Parker?" I looked up from the crate of books I had just packed to find Sadie standing in front of my mother. The blue sleeveless plaid blouse she wore was knotted in the front, exposing part of the white tank top she wore underneath. She looked like the quintessential small-town girl.

"Oh, Sadie!" Mom sounded surprised and relieved to see her. "Yes, of course. Could you give me a hand with this table?" she asked, motioning for Sadie to help her flip it over in order to fold in the legs.

I placed the crate of books in the collapsible shopping cart Mom dragged to Prescott's Grocers once a week when the baskets on her bike wouldn't do. Alex rushed by me so fast that I felt the slightest breeze from him passing. "Mom!" he nearly scolded. "Let me get that!" he insisted.

"Oh, Alex, thank you!" she said, gladly handing the task over. "It's from the library. Can you place it against the wall there so Gail can pick it up in the morning?"

As Alex and Sadie maneuvered the table across the floorboards in squeaking gym shoes, my mother blew the wisps of short blonde hair out of her face, surveying her supplies. "Charli, will you wheel this out the door?"

she asked. Her cheeks grew the slightest shade of pink. "I'll be out in a minute."

With a nod, I obeyed even though I was getting cranky and didn't want to stop at the library before going home. The air was too sticky tonight to walk the extra few blocks.

Luckily, the setting sun cooled the streets and a gentle breeze wiped away some of the impatience and frustration that I had building up as I exited the external doors of the gymnasium. There were a few cars left in the parking lot and some families mingled in the dying daylight.

"Hey, Charli."

I nearly flinched, hearing his voice emerge from the growing shadows before he did. "Geez, Jake," I scolded, a hand over my heart. "You nearly gave me a heart attack!"

A small smile crossed his lips. "Apologies," he said with a hint of humor in his voice.

"What are you still doing here anyway?" I asked. My hand fidgeted with the handle on the shopping cart beside me.

Jake joined me under the security light so that the rest of the world seemed to disappear in the darkening twilight. "Just making sure everyone gets home safe," he said as his eyes quickly scanned the parking lot.

I narrowed my eyebrows at him. "Are you undercover or something?" I asked. I couldn't help the hard rind of irritation I heard on my words.

Jake shook his head. "No. Just doing some... research." He acted as if it was code for something else and before I could ask questions about Ms. Dempsey, Jake changed the subject. "So besides your awesome research and presentation skills, how has your summer been? Are you planning a trip back to the southwest soon?"

The question caught me off guard. I suddenly felt too exposed under the security light. Grabbing the cart, I moved into the shadows of the building, stammering. "What? No. Why would you ask that?"

As my eyes adjusted to the drastically different lighting, Jake followed me deeper into the shadow-drenched parking lot. "Charli, you need—" he started, but was cut off by the metal door of the gymnasium swinging open.

"The campus is now closed. Please see yourselves out before I have to contact the authorities about loitering." Principal Newton's stern voice was clearly agitated as she escorted my mother, Sadie, and Alex out the door. Their faces were painted in guilty expressions.

After Principal Newton closed the security door with an echoing thud, I turned to the trio who had joined us in a vacated parking space. "What did you do?" I asked as if I was their stern-faced mother.

"Why do you—" Sadie started defensively, but Alex cut her off.

"Newton caught these two," Alex explained, pointing to my mother and Sadie, "trying to get into Ms. Dempsey's classroom."

Out of the corner of my eye, I saw Jake's head jerk towards the building. "You do know—" he began, but Sadie was on the defense.

"We weren't trying to get *into* her room," Sadie corrected with a hand on her hip and directed an eye roll at Alex. "We were just curious."

"We just wanted to see if we could get a peek," Mom admitted and nervously adjusted the waistband of her black cotton skirt.

"I mean you did say it was awesome," Sadie said, pointing a finger at me.

Lifting an eyebrow, I narrowed my eyes at her as if to say, *Don't you dare get me involved in this.*

Slicing the tension between Sadie and me, Mom spotted Jake and asked, "Is it true that Ms. Dempsey left a suicide note? What did it say?"

The humidity, mixed with Jake mentioning New Mexico (which brought up unpleasant, frustrated feelings), and Sadie's finger pointing had taken a toll on me. "Let's just go," I blurted, grabbing the handle of the shopping cart and plowed my way through our small circle.

Knowing we had to go to the library, I let my quick pace burn off some of my attitude as I followed the driveway to the front of the school. As I stepped into the bright lamplights of Sheridan Avenue, Alex caught up to me and put a hand on the shopping cart whose metallic clinks and clatters were eating away at my last ounce of patience. "Let me, Charli," he insisted.

Dropping my hand, I let him take it without a word; I didn't want to argue.

We walked in silence as I heard the chatter of my mother and Sadie in the background, not too far behind. "Everything okay, Charli May?" he asked as we passed the corner of Second Street East. His voice was tentative as he tried not to upset me further.

It took several seconds for me to say, "Yeah, fine." I crossed my arms over my chest and blew a lock of my overgrown bangs from my face that had escaped the headband. Honestly, I wasn't okay. Sometimes I'd start to get an anxiety attack that I'd have to punch down so it'd disappear into a tiny pocket of my soul. The littlest things would trigger them; usually it was the small, silly things that I gave up and left behind to move back to Alton Oaks: a quiet Tuesday night on the couch, my own kitchen, air-conditioning, my life...

"Sadie didn't mean anything by—" Alex started.

"I know," I said, my voice softening. Sadie and I had been friends for so long, she knew I wasn't mad at her.

I was just sorting out my mind and soul and needed some space.

Again, Alex and I walked side by side listening to the chatter behind us. It wasn't the gossip that kept me listening, but the distraction from my thoughts. I listened to their newest theory about Ms. Dempsey involving rope burns—which only made me sigh several times, with a series of eye rolls—until we reached the library.

The Alton Oaks library was gorgeous. It sat on the corner of Main Street just before Town Circle. During the day the large windows that faced the river reflected an image of Town Hall amongst the gardens. Several years ago, just after I moved away from home, they renovated the library and added window seats, two cozy fireplaces, and a Shakespeare Garden that my mother still gushes over.

Mom unlocked the front door and disappeared inside with Alex, pulling the cart behind him. A light flipped on inside and illuminated the windows, outlining our silhouettes. I leaned on the back of the green wooden bench along Main Street, grateful that I'd traded Mom's fancy wedges for a pair of flip-flops shortly after my presentation.

"Do you need anything, Charli?" Sadie asked, saddling up beside me. The bench creaked slightly with her weight. "I'm worried about you."

My eyes prickled, threatening to turn on the water works. Swallowing the lump in my throat, I beat down the panic attack. "I'm fine," I lied. "Just tired. And hot."

Sadie knew I was lying, but she didn't press the topic. I was tired of burdening her with my troubles.

Behind us, an employee of the trendy bike store that targeted the out-of-town Canaries was dragging the sidewalk sign along the pavement. The sound of its metal legs scraped across the sidewalk until it hiccupped over the threshold. "Do you want to come over?" Sadie asked. "We could catch up on *American Horror Story* episodes."

It was our favorite television show and the image of us cowering under a blanket on her couch with a half empty bag of chocolate pretzels sounded wonderful— like a marvelous distraction from my problems! "No," I sighed in resignation. I needed to stop getting distracted and deal with my feelings. A chill shook my shoulders with the thought.

Sadie nudged my elbow. Lifting my eyes from a gob of gum on the sidewalk, I saw her smile and couldn't help but return it.

"All right, well, I'm glad that's done," Mom announced as she and Alex exited the library. "Thanks for helping," she said, locking the door and pocketing her keys.

"Where did you hear Ms. Dempsey left a suicide note?" Sadie asked as we began walking towards Oak Street, under the quaintly lit historic part of downtown Alton Oaks. "Because Susan Granger told me otherwise." Susan was a former classmate of ours and the wife of an Alton Oaks police officer. Sadie's voice had conviction; she had a reliable source.

"Oh, you know, I hear things from all over town," Mom shared. I knew she didn't have a source as impressive as Susan Granger since she avoided dropping names. Alex and I exchanged glances that made us roll our eyes in unison as we walked just ahead of the gossiping women. "Supposedly the note said she admitted she failed as a teacher and couldn't go on being mediocre. Sally Fleming said that the note was instead a confession to her fiancé, Lisle; that she wasn't who he thought she was," Mom shared.

"What does that mean?" Sadie asked, taken aback.

Again I snuck a glance at Alex and he shook his head with an exasperated look which made me smile. He kicked a rock down the sidewalk so that it landed just outside the police station which was still brightly lit. We could clearly see the inside of the station as we walked by with officers at their desks, heads hunched over paperwork. It wasn't as busy as it would have been during the day, but having more than one officer on duty this late at night in a town like Alton Oaks was unusual.

"I'm not sure what it means," Mom said in a hushed tone, eying the police station. "Lisle hasn't cried at all from her passing."

"Well, people process grief in different ways," Sadie interjected.

Mom dismissed the comment and continued, "Some people are saying she wasn't as good of a teacher as we thought. That maybe something else was going on."

Our pace caught us up to the rock and I kicked it before Alex could so that it skipped across the concrete and into the darkness outside Mr. Westbrook's Law Offices. "You know, it's not nice to talk about the deceased like that," Alex said, shooting his disapproval with the turn of his head.

Alex and I took a few more turns kicking the rock down Main Street while Sadie and Mom bit their tongues. The corner where we would split up was nearing and I knew they wouldn't make it the rest of the way in silence. It was, after all, the town's Gossip Queen and Little Miss Questions McInquiry.

"Did you meet the janitor?" Sadie asked, barely above a whisper. Mom must've shaken her head because Sadie continued, "I tried to ask him for more paper towels in the kitchen tonight, but he completely ignored me. What's up with that?"

Mom was eager to answer. "Well, I heard—"

"Well, we'll see you guys later. Will you make it home okay?" Alex cut in as we stood under the lamp post outside the bank on the corner of Oak and Main.

The corner of Mom's lip dipped momentarily when Alex stole her audience just by draping his arm around Sadie. "Yeah, we'll be fine," I assured him, putting a hand on Mom's elbow to nudge her towards Oak Street.

With polite, small-town manners, Mom smiled and waved goodbye after giving Alex a hug, but she was dying to finish her sentence, to talk to someone who would engage in town gossip.

Silently, we walked up Oak Street and Mom sighed several times. Minutes seemed to stretch into hours as our feet began dragging across the pavement and bats swooped above us, gobbling up the hovering insects. When the Kratsky house came into view, with its front room lights burning a hole into the night, Mom waved to Mrs. Kratsky who sat in her chair by the window and said, "I'll be home in a bit. Go on ahead without me, Charli," and ran up the stairs before I got a chance to say goodbye.

CHAPTER FIVE

Friday morning had an electrifying buzz in the air, despite the still growing humidity; it was the last Friday of the school year, the entryway to the last weekend before summer vacation. The sun had risen at five o'clock that morning, and its rays grew more fierce as I walked down Oak Street. Originally, I was supposed to spend the remainder of this week shadowing Ms. Dempsey since I'd be working with a number of her students during the summer classes. Now, however, I didn't know what to expect when I walked into the school.

As I cut across the parking lot to the south end of the building, I could already see a number of students on the playground. There were some adults—parents with bright yellow *Visitor* passes pinned to their shirts— monitoring the playground and the parking lot for student safety.

Just as I walked past a white Chevy Malibu, the driver's door swung open, nearly clotheslining me to the ground. "Oh, I am so sorry!" A woman wearing a white pencil skirt and an airy black blouse climbed out of the driver's seat and put a hand on my arm. "Are you all right?" she asked. "That was completely my fault; I wasn't paying attention."

Realizing that no part of my body was screaming out in pain, I straightened up and looked at the woman— her short nappy hair was spiked in little tufts on her head and the long fake pearl necklace brought out her dark skin and brown eyes. "I'm fine. No worries," I ensured her, smiling. "We all have a lot on our minds lately."

The woman frowned momentarily and swung the strap of her purse over her shoulder. "I'm Willa Corden," she introduced. "I teach sixth grade here." She extended her hand and gave me a firm handshake, the skin on her palm was rough and dry despite the moisture in the air. "You're Charlotte Parker, right? I loved the speech you gave last night."

"Thank you," I said, pleased with the compliment. "Please call me Charli."

Willa nodded then reached into her backseat for a crate of binders, books, and papers. She placed it on the blacktop of the parking lot and then extended a handle from the base in order to wheel it into the building. "I've been a teacher here for four years, and I never knew any of that Alton Oaks history before, which I'm ashamed of—I'm the history teacher!" she admitted, closing and locking her car.

"Really?" I asked, not too shocked. With each passing year, more and more of our history gets lost.

We began to walk to the south end of the school as the echoes from the playground bounced off the buildings. Willa shook her head and lowered her voice, "It's not part of the standards—the history of Alton Oaks—so Newton doesn't really approve." I nodded, understanding. Principal Newton seemed to be like many of the nation's school administrators who looked at data and numbers instead of the child and their world. I certainly did not miss that.

"Justin!" Willa's change in tone caught me off guard as she called to a young boy on the edge of the playground. She marched right up to the boy in her gold flats with the authority of a teacher.

Hanging back, I let my nosy Alton blood take over and eavesdropped. "Justin Willkens!" Willa stated his name again, standing a few yards from where he stood. A group of three young boys stood around him, looking up as he lit leaves on fire with a lighter.

Justin looked up and his body language dripped with attitude as he dramatically sighed and trudged towards Willa while the younger boys scattered back to the playground. "What now?" Justin asked, his voice poking at Willa like a needle to a water balloon.

Willa held out her hand. "Justin, how many of these do I have to confiscate from you?" She pocketed the lighter immediately after he dropped it in her hand. "Fire is not something to play around with, especially with first graders. I'm going to have to write you up for this. I will contact the junior high principal—you can't keep doing this, Justin."

Justin hunched over, his hands in the pockets of his baggy faded jeans and his dingy t-shirt clung to his back; it was full of the dirt and teenage sweat that never fully washed away in the laundry.

The sun beat down on us and I squinted, holding my hand to my forehead to block the glare of the sun, still low in the eastern sky. "Whatever," Justin spat. "I'll just get another one."

"Maybe we should have a conference with your parents then?" Willa suggested.

Justin became aggressive in his stance. His weight bounced from foot to foot and he couldn't decide what to do with his hands "Man, I thought life would get easier with Ms. Dempsey gone, now I gotta worry about you?"

From where I stood, even I could see that Justin had touched a nerve in Willa. She stood with a hand on her hip as she said, "Your parents will be getting a personal phone call from me today, have no doubt about that, Justin. Until then, I think it wise you keep your nose clean."

Justin scoffed and kicked a rock on the edge of the parking lot. "Whatever," he responded.

As Willa walked back to where I stood with her crate of paperwork, she took the time to calm her nerves and return to normal. "Sorry about that," she said as she grabbed the handle of her crate. "That's Justin Willkens," she began to explain as we walked towards the entrance of the building. "He's always up to something. I wouldn't mind so much if he was at least constructive, but no."

I held open the door to the school's entrance for Willa and a blast of cold air met us, licking away the beads of sweat that had gathered in the morning sun. "Dee—Ms. Dempsey—she would always catch him doing things outside of her classroom window, which is in front of the playground. Things like pushing kids, relieving himself on the building, throwing rocks, uprooting plants in her classroom garden. He's a seventh grader at the junior high but always hangs out over here."

Before Willa could continue, the front desk receptionist, a fresh out-of-high-school girl named Brittney, appeared. "Hey, Charli," she said.

"Sorry for talking your ear off—and for almost hitting you with my car door," Willa apologized. "I hope to see you around campus, Charli. Good luck today!" she said before disappearing through the door beside the receptionist's desk.

"Hi, Brittney," I greeted, picking up the blue pen with a bright pink flower taped to the top. "What's the official countdown to summer break?" I asked signing into the visitor's log.

"Five days and counting!" she said, sorting through the papers on her desk. "Looks like Principal Newton has a schedule for you today," Brittney reported, handing me an index card with a timetable printed on it.

"You know where all the rooms are?" she asked.

My eyes traveled down the list: from nine to ten-thirty I would shadow-slash-substitute for Kindergarten, eat lunch while observing behavior on the playground during the two recess shifts from ten-thirty to noon, and then finish the day shadowing Willa Corden in the sixth grade. I suddenly wondered if my role for summer classes was changing, but figured I'd rather step in and help where I could instead of having to talk to Principal Newton again.

"Yeah, I got it. Thanks, Brittney," I said, pocketing the card and walking through the door beside her desk.

"Good luck!" she called after me just as the phone began to ring.

I had forgotten how exhausting (but fun!) it was to be inside a classroom again. It had only been two months since I left my job in Albuquerque, but I was out of shape. My feet hurt, I was dehydrated, and I really had to use the bathroom.

At the end of the day, when I was ready for a shower and nap, Principal Newton stuck her head into the receptionist's office as I was signing out on the visitor's log. "Come see me before you leave," she instructed, slipping a file folder into the mailbox outside her office door. I had only known her for two days, but I already had a feeling of dread when she asked me to come into her office.

Her room had the overpowering smell of a new floral air freshener. The wood paneled walls choked on the sunlight that climbed through the yellow blinds. She moved a binder to the neatly organized row of filing cabinets behind her and motioned for me to sit in one of the wooden chairs in front of her meticulously kept desk.

"How did it go today?" she asked, folding her hands

and placing them on the desk in front of her.

The cool air of her air-conditioned office, and the fact that it was the first time I'd sat all day, made me suddenly exhausted, despite the hardness of the chair under me. "Pretty well," I shared, shuffling slightly in the chair.

Principal Newton showed no emotion, but studied me for several uncomfortable seconds. "Did I do something wrong?" I asked, feeling like a kid in the principal's office.

Without answering my question, Principal Newton replied, "As you know, school is out for the summer on Wednesday. Would you be interested in helping out here and there until then? We still have four full days of learning to utilize and the loss of Ms. Dempsey has affected our academic growth."

Squirming in the uncomfortable chair, I bit my tongue at her lack of empathy. Besides, the last week of school was about reflection, community, and celebration, or at least they used to be.

"Sure," I agreed. I wasn't about to turn down a paycheck and a possible reference, especially after the hasty departure from my last school.

"Excellent," Principal Newton said and extended her hand. As I shook her surprisingly soft palm, she instructed, "Be here at 6:45 tomorrow morning so I can review the handbook with you; there are a few—"

She was cut off by the door to her office flying open and slamming into the wall, rattling the framed degrees and awards that hung nearby. I jumped, startled, and gripped the wooden arm of the chair as I turned.

A dark-haired man in old-fashioned tortoise shell print glasses appeared, gripping the door frame. His face was red and splotchy, either from the pain of grief or the fire of alcohol. "You!" he exclaimed with pain searing his voice. His hand, shaking slightly, pointed directly at Principal Newton.

Principal Newton looked up as if such dramatic displays were an everyday occurrence. "Lyle," she said as if dealing with him was going to be a chore that was beneath her.

"It's your fault!" he exclaimed, moving closer to her desk. "She was a perfectly perfect person." His face momentarily lost its angry shell and showed raw pain. "And you did nothing but push her around!"

"If you'll excuse us," Principal Newton said, her arm extended, showing me the way out.

More than happy to leave her office, I cautiously squeezed past the angry man, leaving them alone. "You won't get away with it!" the man yelled as I made a beeline for the building's exit. "As long as I live and breathe, you will never get away with it!" he yelled and the echo followed me out the door.

CHAPTER SIX

Walking across the now empty parking lot, I kept turning back to the school, hoping Principal Newton would be all right. Just to be sure, I sent a quick text to Jake and asked him to check on the situation.

As I strolled up Oak Street, the sun beat down on the landscape and I felt it slightly burn the skin of my bare shoulders. Passing the Kratsky's house, I heard banging come from Mr. K.'s workshop and imagined how busy he was since Alton Oaks' 28th Annual Bicycle Race was a mere three weeks ago. I'm sure a lot of bicycles needed tuning.

The sound of a lawn mower traveled through the late afternoon air with the scent of a faraway barbeque. Ahead, I could just see Rip Oakley, Alton Oak's newest resident, in a t-shirt and jeans, pushing a lawn mower across his property. He'd soon learn that living this far outside town, with that much land, a riding lawn mower is worth the investment.

When I got closer, he killed the engine with a smile and wiped his brow. "Hey, neighbor," he greeted.

When he'd first moved to Alton Oaks, we had a rocky start as neighbors, but we began to grow on each other. "Hey," I replied. "Busy day?"

Rip had been working nonstop at remodeling that old house and it was coming along nicely. Since I was a kid, the house had stood empty and collected dust, mold, and rot. When I was researching Alton Oaks' history for my presentation, I'd learned that Rip's house was nearly as old as ours. The Alton House, however, was in much better shape, which says a lot. It was probably cheaper to tear down the house and build a new one on the land, but for some reason Rip really liked that old place. And while Rip worked hard at gutting the inside, contractors had just finished installing white aluminum siding and a new roof on its outside.

Rip shrugged. "Finished the tile flooring in the kitchen; it's gettin' there."

"Didn't you just finish installing new cabinets? When do you sleep?" I asked. Gnats were flying above my head and I swatted them away, moving aside.

He laughed half-heartedly and changed the subject. "I wanted to tell you that I enjoyed your speech at the school last night," he said, squinting his eyes in the sunlight.

"You were there?" I asked. It surprised me that he had taken the time to attend since he had no kids or family in town that I knew of, and Heritage Night was usually a school event for students and their families. People normally didn't go for the fun of it.

Shrugging, he replied, "History interests me. I had no idea how dramatic this town's history was."

I nodded. "Did you know that there's an urban legend that Andrew Alton's ghost wanders through town looking for D. B. Williams or his murderer?"

Rip considered this and leaned his head in thought. He then replied, "They could be the same person."

I shrugged, feeling the tightness of sunburn on my shoulders. "Either way, it always was taboo to invite his great-great-granddaughter to any sleepover parties for fear that his ghost would accompany her." Okay, maybe that wasn't 100% true. In fact, only one person ever told me that, but she was surrounded by eight other girls who had their arms folded over their chest and who had nodded judgmentally in agreement.

"Well, I think it's cool," he said, picking up a branch that had fallen from a nearby tree and dragged it closer to the house.

In the distance, the screen door of the Alton house screeched open and slammed against its frame. Eli burst out of the house and began running around on the front lawn. "You might be the only one who thinks so," I remarked. "Ever."

His laugh was more genuine this time. Mrs. Kratsky's *hee-haw* golf cart horn sounded as she passed by. Rip and I waved and watched as she parked in the Alton driveway and climbed the stairs to join my mother and sister on the porch.

Rip looked from the porch of women to me and bent down to start the motor again. "I'll catch you later, Charli," he said and the roar of the lawn mower burst any potential further conversation.

When I reached the front steps, my mother's gossip club was in full swing, even my cousin Jenna had flown over from her house next door. Their heads popped up as my exhausted feet clobbered on to the creaking stairs. "Charli! Come sit here," my sister Bailey said, patting the space on the bench beside her.

Bailey and I were never really close and it wasn't because of an age old fight or sibling rivalry; we were just different people and no matter how hard we tried, we couldn't understand each other. I know her invitation was a genuine gesture to include me in the gossip, but the drama didn't interest me. Honestly, all I wanted was a shower, and maybe a glass of wine.

Nevertheless, my sister was trying so I should too. I sat down with an empty smile. After comparing gossip on the Burbanks' new boat and the fight between Larry Proust and Bill McGuire about property lines, Jenna turned to me and asked, "How do you like it so far at the school, Charli?"

All eyes were on me and I knew where this line of questioning was going to go: Ms. Dempsey's suicide. There was no way getting out of this so I shrugged. "The teachers are nice. I've missed working with kids."

Jenna nodded, understanding. She had been working with children of all abilities since college, more than sixteen years ago. Jenna's husband, Mark, was a high school science teacher. When they found out they couldn't have children, they dedicated their lives to their work. "They're a great bunch," she added. "How are Dee's kids holding up?"

"Dee?" I asked.

"Ms. Dempsey," Jenna corrected. "We all called her Dee. Are the kids doing okay?"

There it is. My mother, Mrs. Kratsky, Bailey, and Jenna all leaned in slightly with this topic. Of course, I had a talent for being in the wrong place at the wrong time like last April, when Sara Zimmer's murder was the talk of the town, and I think they all expected some inside details from me about Ms. Dempsey.

"I didn't really get to see her class today, I was mainly with Kindergarten and sixth grade," I shared. Then I thought about those sun-filled hours on the playground where I was a monitor who really wished she had brought a frozen water bottle and a hat with her. There were a few kids during the last recess session who were sluggish and sat on the wrap-around bench under the large oak tree. I had shrugged off their behavior due to the heat of the day, but maybe they were nursing a heartache for their teacher.

"It's a shame about Ms. Dempsey," Mrs. Kratsky chimed in, shaking her head.

"Very shameful," my sister spat as if she was being attacked. "Of all the places to commit suicide, she chose her classroom? If she was such a great teacher, why would she have done that in a place her students considered safe and happy? Did she realize the implications for her students' mental health?" Bailey was very upset. She balled her hand into a fist and lightly pounded it onto her knee as she talked.

I'll admit that Bailey had a point. Not only was Ms. Dempsey about to get married, but I couldn't believe that she would hurt her children by hanging herself in her own classroom. I suddenly got a bad feeling that our town had another murder on its hands.

"Well, Sandy, down at the post office, she told me that all the junior high kids think the janitor did it," my mother shared.

"Why would he do that?" I asked. I admit he seemed a bit invisible and stuck to the shadows at the Heritage Fair, but he seemed like a nice guy when I saw him in the halls during the school day. He was just a bit shy.

Mom shrugged from her place on the porch swing and gripped a glass of iced tea. The remaining ice cubes clinked against the glass with the movement. "There could be a number of reasons, Charli," she said. She then lifted an eyebrow and asked, "What do you think?"

My mother was still a smidge upset that I'd neglected to share key details of Sara Zimmer's murder that would have upped her gossip game. I knew I was in for a rollercoaster of questioning for any hot topic that transpired in my proximity. "I don't know," I said, feeling that Bailey's gaze was too close. "I don't know him, but he seems like an okay guy," I said, hoping it was enough to take the attention off of me.

"So I heard something that I'm not quite sure is something," Mrs. Kratsky said from the wooden rocking chair. She had been fanning herself with an envelope that she had pulled from the waistband of her skirt. "I heard it down at The Buzz, so make of it what you will." Mrs. Kratsky paused, knowing she had everyone's full attention. "I overheard someone say that the knot on Ms. Dempsey's rope was a double overhand knot. Now, I don't know one knot from another, but apparently when the crime scene unit went through her classroom, they found the last entry on her search engine was how to tie a double overhand knot."

I heard at least one gasp from the women surrounding me. "Not only that, but the search before it was the hangman's knot," Mrs. Kratsky added.

Bailey tisked loudly and looked over at Eli who was pretending to fight an invisible monster on the front lawn. "It sounds like," my mother interjected, "that this woman had a lot more going on in her life than what others saw."

"Those poor kids," Jenna said, shaking her head.

My mother's phone chimed, stealing us from our own thoughts. "Sorry, ladies," Mom said. "There's a fundraising event at the library at 7:30 tonight, so I have to duck out and get ready."

Mrs. Kratsky, despite her aging bones, jumped out of the rocking chair spryly. "I will see you there, Rose. Can't wait to play!" As Mom and Mrs. Kratsky walked across the porch, talking about which CLUE character they were dressing up as for the real-life murder mystery game that the library was putting on, Bailey called for Eli.

Eli was still wary of me. Before I moved back to Alton Oaks I had seen him only three times and now I was just the strange lady who lived next door with Grandma and Grandpa. As Bailey instructed Eli to say goodbye to our mother, she turned and said, "Now say goodbye to Auntie Charli!"

Usually he'd get shy and refuse to, but today he had his hands balled into fists and jerked them in front of him while, in a measured, superhero-like voice replied, "Good bye, Earthling!"

Bailey raised her eyebrows while she shuffled him to

the porch stairs in her flip-flops. I considered that exchange progress in our aunt-nephew relationship.

After a shower, I walked downstairs in pajamas—okay, a pair of old volleyball shorts and a tank top that had a small rip under my left arm, I was never one for matching pajamas or nightgowns like Bailey. Walking into the quiet kitchen, I could see that night had almost fallen. The sound of crickets traveled through the kitchen windows while the box fan in the dining room window hummed itself awake.

Tearing a limb from the aloe plant above the kitchen sink, I squeezed the gel onto my sunburned shoulders and immediately felt relieved. The house was getting stuffy from the lingering heat of the day and I decided to eat my dinner—a complex meal of peanut butter and graham crackers—on the porch. Since no one was home, it would be a relaxing hour or so to myself.

Before I left the airless house, I grabbed a frozen juice box from the freezer (Mom liked to keep them around for Eli). With a pair of scissors, I cut open the top to reveal the slushy drink inside. Feeling a bit impish, I reached above the fridge and grabbed a dusty bottle of tequila. A bit heavy-handedly, I tipped the bottle over my slushy, added the straw, and walked onto the front porch happily, as if I was getting away with something forbidden.

After devouring half the box of graham crackers, I lounged on the porch swing, sipping my faux-margarita through a straw and watched the fireflies dance around the yard in the rising moonlight. Contentment washed over me as still-damp strands of my hair fell onto my warm shoulders and I watched a flashing bicycle headlight travel up Oak Street.

Then, on the patio table in front of the porch swing, next to the crumbs of my dinner, my cell phone started to vibrate. For the past two months I'd feared the ringing of my phone. My stomach would cringe and twinge, my forehead would wrinkle in anxiety and something inside me would cry out in a full-on panic. I dreaded looking at my screen to see that Jackson was calling. Yes, it had been two months since I'd walked out on him, but I still wasn't ready to talk to him; I didn't know what to say.

Usually, though, I'd work myself up for nothing because it was Sadie calling, or my cousin Jillian, or my brother Alex. Taking a deep breath and telling myself it was just Sadie, I picked up my phone and turned it over.

Jackson.

The butterflies in my stomach turned to claws churning in acid. I slid my finger across the screen to ignore his call. Holding the phone in my hand, I stared at my reflection in the blackness that, only a few seconds ago, was brightly lit with his name and picture. Where did our happiness go? What happened to our relationship? What did I do wrong? My overgrown bangs were pinned to the side of my head so I could clearly see the tears welling beneath my green eyes.

"Hello? Charlotte? Hello?"

My eyes widened upon hearing Jackson's voice. Sitting up, I realized that I probably answered the call instead of ignoring it.

"Charlotte? Are you there?"

I put the phone to my ear but couldn't say anything. I heard noises in the background—a television? Radio? People?

Panicking, I held the phone out in front of me and held down the power button until the manufacturer's melody and logo blazoned and then faded off the screen. I held it, at arm's length, and watched my reflection in the screen, afraid that he would still be on the line.

"Are you okay, Charli?"

Looking up, I saw Jake at the top of the porch stairs in his brown deputy uniform. "You're white as a sheet," he said, making his way over to the porch swing.

Moving aside the box of graham crackers and the melted remnants of my grown-up juice box, Jake sat down across from me on the patio table, the metal legs scraped across the floor slightly as he did. "Geez, Charli, you look like you've seen a ghost," he commented, putting a hand on my arm.

I immediately shook off his warm hand. His brown eyes searched my face for a clue as to what had happened. I felt tears puddling behind my eyes and really wished Jake wasn't there. "I just need a minute," I said, putting up one finger and turning away from him.

I knew I needed to deal with Jackson, I really did. I had to deal with these emotions and tell him exactly how hurt I was. Determine whether or not we had a future, and what my future was going to be. To figure out what *I* wanted. But as I let the tears fall down my cheeks, I buried my face in my hands, not yet strong enough to accomplish any of these tasks.

"Charli?" Jake's voice was quiet as he tentatively placed a hand on my back.

"I'm fine. Just... a minute," I said trying to dam up the river of hurt.

"Is it him?" Jake asked. No one in Alton Oaks quite knew my story, not even my mother. Sadie knew my soul, so she had pieced together most of the story without having to ask.

With the heels of my palms, I rubbed my eyes and let the air evaporate any trace of moisture as I dropped my hands into my lap. "No, I'm fine," I said, not yet ready to face Jake. I took a few long, deep breaths as I watched the tops of the oak trees sway in the moonlit breeze.

"Charli," he began with a more pointed tone, "you have to do something about it or it'll eat at you."

Jake was opening a door for a conversation about Jackson and I wanted to slam it shut, bolt it down, and bury it immediately. Turning to face him, I put on a smile and replied in a too-cheery tone, "I'm fine. What brings you by, Jake?" I asked pulling my legs up to sit crisscross on the swing.

I could see it in his eyes that he weighed whether or not to broach the subject again or to change it completely. Finally, with a hint of disappointment, he said, "Nothing, Charli." He sighed and moved to sit on the bench beneath the window. "I just saw your porch light on and thought I'd see how you were doing. You were pretty shook up when you left the school last night."

"Yeah, I'm okay. Thanks, Jake." I smiled, looking briefly in his direction. I found it hard to look him in the eye for too long after he had witnessed my small breakdown. "You probably can't talk about it, but how are things going for Ms. Dempsey's case?" Thinking Jake was arriving home later than usual, I looked at my wrist to check the time, only to discover my watch was probably still sitting on the bathroom counter.

Probably taking pity on me, Jake was more willing to share what little information he had. "We're waiting on the autopsy report. It should be in by tomorrow morning at the earliest, but I'm not holding my breath."

In the distance, the sound of a motorcycle roared through the darkness. I assumed it was Rip and somewhere down the road he was pulling out of his driveway. "It's still hard to believe that now Alton Oaks has to deal with a suicide on top of what happened to Sara in April."

Jake said nothing and nodded. He was looking down at the table, his thoughts in another world. An owl hooted in the distance and I picked at a hangnail. "Can I ask you a question?" I asked suddenly. The questions buzzing around my head needed some answers.

Jake merely looked up from the table.

"Between you and me," I started in a hushed tone, leaning towards him, "is it true about her computer? The search engine results?"

His eyes flitted left and then right, making sure we were alone, before giving me a curt nod.

It still didn't sit right with me that a teacher who dedicated her life to her students would commit suicide in her classroom. "Are you sure? Are you sure it was her computer? Her fingerprints are on the keyboard and everything?"

Jake's eyes met mine and he pursed his lips.

"I just don't get it," I said, pushing my damp hair over my shoulder, momentarily wincing as my fingertips scratched across the sunburn. "Why would she do that before hanging herself? Why would she do it in her classroom?" Something about the situation didn't sit right with me.

Jake sat with his chin resting on his hands, staring into the yard. "Charli," he finally said, holding my eyes. "Between you and me," he leaned in closer and spoke barely above a whisper. He paused for so long that, for a moment, I thought he had changed his mind and wasn't going to finish his sentence. "Between you and me, I don't think this was a suicide. There were no fingerprints on her keyboard. They had been wiped clean."

CHAPTER SEVEN

The next day I walked to the elementary school at six in the morning to review the handbook with Principal Newton, only to discover I was wearing inappropriate shoes and the pink chiffon blouse I had worn over a tank top was considered "too revealing." By the end of the day I was feeling as beat down as the students who were taking their last reading fluency exams of the year.

During the last hour of the day, I was sitting at a small desk, armed with a stopwatch and test booklets, staring at the door at the far end of the hallway: Ms. Dempsey's room. I was tasked to pull each one of Ms. Dempsey's students, one-by-one, and have them read three different texts while I timed them and checked for accuracy.

Thirty yards outside their old classroom.

Where their teacher was found dead.

Two days ago.

It was not a pleasant task.

During my time in and out of the bland classroom with the plump, grey-haired, no-nonsense substitute, I noticed that one girl, in particular, was having a rough day. She sat with her head in her arms and looked out the window, barely noticing the environment around her. When I called her out into the hallway, her eyes were red and I could tell she wasn't handling her teacher's demise very well. "Lindy?" I said, tapping her on the shoulder. "Come out into the hall with me for a while," I instructed.

Her chair dragged across the linoleum and she followed me, lumbering out the door.

Plopping into the wooden chair, she stared at the test booklet in front of her. "Okay, Lindy," I said in the softest voice I could muster. "I'm going to give you three minutes to read the text aloud. When I say stop, you close the booklet. Understand?" I asked, unable to catch her gaze.

Her fingers played with the corner of the test packet. "Okay. You may open the packet and begin when I say 'Go.' Ready?" Still, no response from the child.

"Go," I stated and started the stopwatch.

Lindy only sat in the chair, playing with the corner of the pages. I looked up and down the hallway and strained my ears for the *clack-clack* sound of Principal Newton's shoes. When I deemed the coast clear, I stopped the clock and cleared it. "Would you like to see the counselor?" I asked, unsure of how to approach the child.

She shrugged without looking up. Her straight, dirty-blonde hair fell in front of her face as she slouched in the chair. It wasn't until I saw a tear splash onto her hand that I noticed she was crying. "What's the point?" she asked in a mousy voice.

Tentatively, I engaged in a conversation. "The counselor can help you talk about what's bothering you."

Lindy dropped her hand into her lap and fiddled with the zipper on her brown sleeveless hoodie. "It won't bring Ms. Dempsey back," she said almost in a pout.

I bit my bottom lip. Again I looked left and right. I put the stopwatch and pencil down on the table. "I was about your age when I lost my grandma," I shared. "She would take me for rides in her canoe on the river so early in the morning, you could see dreams floating out of the windows of the people waking up. She told me I could do anything—be anything I wanted; she even bought me my first camera. I loved her more than anything and when she died I thought my world had ended."

Lindy looked up at me from above her purple framed glasses. I continued, "My teacher sent me to the school counselor because I was so sad. And he said that talking about all the good things my grandma did with me would help me."

Several moments passed and I wondered if I did more harm than good. Finally, Lindy sat up a bit in her chair and said, "Ms. Dempsey is.. was—*is* my favorite teacher. She would listen to me, like *really* listen. In the beginning of the year she caught me drawing a goblin on the corner of my math paper and I thought I was in trouble. She took the paper from me and gave me a new math sheet. I waited all day thinking she was going to punish me or tell my parents. The next day I came to school and there was a brand new sketchbook on my desk, she cut out the goblin and posted it on the first page and wrote a story to go with it.

"So every once in a while I'd leave a drawing on her desk and she'd write a short little story to go with it and leave it on my desk. No one ever did anything like that with me before. She didn't make me hide my drawings or yell at me for them." Lindy grew quiet as a fresh batch of silent tears fell down her cheeks.

"And since Christmas I've been working on a book for Ms. Dempsey. I drew pictures and this time I wrote the story that went with them; about a goblin who lives in our class garden. I was going to give it to her the last day of school, but..." Lindy cried into her hands and I wished I could pull her into a hug, but according to the Employee Handbook I was lectured on this morning, it was not allowed.

My heart ached for the pain this eleven year old girl

was going through. I knelt down beside her and put my arm around her shoulder. "It's okay to cry," I reassured her as she shook with tears.

"You know what I think?" I asked, several minutes later when she had calmed down.

"What?" she asked, her word coated in anguish.

"I think Ms. Dempsey was a wonderful teacher."

"You didn't even know her," Lindy said defensively.

"No, I didn't. You're right," I agreed. "But I know the effect she had on her students. And a great teacher like that should be remembered the right way."

Lindy's lips danced from one side of her mouth to the other. "And what way is that?" she asked a bit haughtily.

"How does any teacher want to be remembered?" I asked. Lindy answered in silence, so I continued, "A piece of her lives on in each of her students. Let Ms. Dempsey shine through your drawings and your stories; I think she'd like that."

Lindy thought about it and wiped her eyes with the lining of her hoodie. "May I use the bathroom before we start this test? I think Ms. Dempsey would want me to try and do my best."

Smiling with relief, I answered, "Of course you may."

As I wrote Lindy a pass and watched her disappear down the hallway, I stared at Ms. Dempsey's door, with the children's art work still covering the window, and knew, deep down, she did not kill herself.

CHAPTER EIGHT

As dismissal was in full swing—children wandering the hallways carrying projects, paper, and poster board—I stopped in the front office to see if I was clear to sign out for the day. After all, it was Friday and I had been having an emotional day; I wanted to clear out of there.

"Am I good to go?" I asked Brittany, who was handing a parent a file folder over the partition.

"She wants to see you," Brittany said in a lower voice and nodded towards the closed door of Principal Newton's office.

Taking a deep breath, I checked my clothes and hair for anything she might find wrong. I lifted my hand to knock on the door when Principal Newton opened it. "Oh, Charli, you're here. Good. Follow me," she instructed. "I need you to help pack up some of Ms. Dempsey's belongings. Her fiancé will be coming by to pick them up," she explained as we made our way to the gym.

Clack-clack went her shoes as we walked across the wooden floor. "Honestly, she should have had the decency to do this before she..." Principal Newton stopped herself from finishing that sentence, thankfully.

As we walked into the hallway, the janitor was just leaving Ms. Dempsey's room. He was searching the ring of keys on his belt when he looked up and saw us approach. "No need, Walter," Principal Newton said. "You can keep it unlocked for now."

He nodded and attached the key ring back to his belt.

"I trust you left the boxes, like I instructed?" Principal Newton asked, grabbing onto the doorknob.

"Yes, ma'am," Walter said without making eye contact. His cart was parked against the wall and he pushed it to the nearest garbage can. I watched as he meticulously changed the lining and emptied it into his cart.

"Charli," Principal Newton's voice was impatient. "Let's go," she said, holding the door open to a colorful world many teachers (and children) only dream about.

Inside, on the horseshoe-shaped table, many flattened cardboard boxes sat towering with a roll of packing tape beside it. "I need you to start packing up Ms. Dempsey's belongings. Her fiancé will be here any minute; he'll come through the external door here," Principal Newton shared as she took out a set of keys and unlocked the door behind Ms. Dempsey's desk.

Not sure where to start, I asked, "What's hers? What do I pack?"

Principal Newton walked towards the door we had just entered. "If it's colorful or looks like it doesn't belong in a classroom, it's hers." Before closing the door behind her, she added, "You may sign out at four o'clock, but please get as much done as you can."

With the thump-click of the closing door, I stood alone in the classroom. A shiver ran through me thinking about what had happened not forty-eight hours ago. Staying clear of Ms. Dempsey's desk, I walked around the room in awe of its organization and resources.

The desks were clumped into tables, where red, blue, and yellow yoga balls sat beneath them—not one desk was isolated into an island, which I was impressed with because there was always that one child who needed his own space in order for the teacher to get anything done. Wire shelves with cloth bins stood at one end of each table clump, filled with supplies, and a garbage can at the other end. At the top of each shelf sat a laminated list of jobs where the students signed up for weekly tasks.

Ms. Dempsey's classroom was in the corner of the building so she had windows on two walls, which let in a lot of natural light. On the south end there was a view of the baseball field and basketball court, and vegetation grew on the ledge below the window. As I walked by, an earthy scent filled my lungs with a hint of dill and oregano. Pots painted by children held various herbs and old egg cartons growing seedlings that I assumed would be planted in the raised garden bed below the window, outside.

The east wall had a view of the playground and part of the parking lot while several student projects hung on a clothesline that showcased student work: book reports, test grades, creative stories, and so on. Several bookcases lined the space below the windows and held books, color-coded by genre. I marveled at the wall space to the north where Ms. Dempsey kept line graphs of student achievement based on the skill they were covering in math. It outlined a class goal (70% of the class would pass the post-assessment with a 75% or above) and a class reward for meeting the goal (a class picnic on the football field). Even the full size skeleton was arranged to point at it with one hand and give a thumbs up with the other. She even had a *Jobs Wanted* board where her students could apply and interview for classroom jobs!

And, the whiteboard that covered the western wall of the room, had been sectioned it off in black-and-daisy printed tape that held a *Word of the Week*—which was written in English, Spanish, French, and in Chinese characters, an inspirational quote written in the scratchy, unsure handwriting of a child, a Math

Challenge problem, and a Journal Prompt. Then, in block letters the schedule for the day was posted, each objective and standard clearly defined under each block of time, and the date was scrawled above it—June 1, 2016. I bit my lip, staring at her neat, purple, whiteboard-marker writing, wondering why she would have prepared the following day's schedule if she did not plan on being there.

"What are you doing here?" a deeply congested voice asked, seemingly taking offense to my presence.

Turning around, I saw the man with the tortoise-shell glasses who'd stormed into the principal's office yesterday. Today, however, his brown hair was neatly combed to the side and his face was blank like a sheet of paper, not red and distressed. He stood in the open frame of the external door, letting drafts of warm, humid air into the room, holding a large box in his hands.

"Sorry, I'm Charli," I replied, walking towards Ms. Dempsey's desk, where he had placed the box. He slipped his glasses back up his nose with one finger and watched me, either unimpressed or impatient with me already. "Principal Newton asked me to help pack up Ms. Dempsey's belongs," I added.

"Well, what a fine job you've done," he said, his eyes hard and unforgiving. "Besides, I don't need any help. I can take care of my fiancé's belongings myself."

"Oh, behave, Lyle," instructed a woman squeezing through the door. She too held a box and Lyle moved aside, deeper into the corner behind the desk, to accommodate her. "I'm Veronica," she greeted, extending a hand and balancing the box between the desk and her ripped jeans. Her eyes were slightly swollen as if she had recently been crying. "Thank you for your help."

The woman placed the box on the ground and wiped

her hands on her faded red, St. Louis Cardinals t-shirt. Looking from her to Lyle, I responded, "It's no problem. I'm sorry about your loss. I could tell she was a great teacher." I grabbed a flattened box from the horseshoe table and began to assemble it.

Veronica was unpacking tape, garbage bags, and other supplies from her box on the desk while Lyle sulked in the corner. "Thank you," she said.

Lyle picked up a picture frame that sat on Ms. Dempsey's desk and, rather upset, remarked, "Great? No. She was wonderful. You people couldn't see that."

Veronica turned and put a hand on Lyle's arm. "Lyle, please," she pleaded.

Lyle shook off her arm and, with tears pooling in his eyes, said to her, "That no good principal—how am I supposed to just live with this?"

"I know, Lyle, but now isn't the time," she said in a hushed tone, briefly turning to me with a forced smile and then redirected her attention to Lyle. I pretended to be extremely interested in taping my box together.

Lyle looked past Veronica and caught me sneaking a peek at them from the corner of my eye. In a much sharper tone he said to me, "Did you know your boss, that scum principal, threatened to fire Dee? All she did was love these children and give them a safe place. She made them want to learn—made it fun. She taught kids to want to learn, which is more important than a stupid test score."

"Lyle, please," Veronica pleaded once more as he walked in front of the desk.

"No," he spat. "Do you know how many weekends and plans she canceled to work for this school? Do you know how many nights I ate alone because she was working on the school newspaper or art club—both of which the principal tried to shut down? No. Dee worked too hard to be remembered like this."

Veronica came up behind him and gently grabbed his elbow. Snapping out of his angry trance, he whipped his head to Veronica, a tear escaping and rolling down his cheek, "I can't do this, Ronnie. I'm not ready."

She put an arm around his shoulder and in hushed words led him to the door.

As I was taping up my fifth cardboard box, Veronica closed the door behind Lyle. "I'm sorry," she said, leaning against the door for a moment. "Please forgive him."

Placing an empty box on the floor, I put down the packing tape. "It's okay," I said. "I completely understand."

Veronica walked over to the horseshoe table and picked up an empty box. "They were going to be married in two weeks," she admitted as emotion wrinkled her face. "He knows she couldn't have killed herself. It beats him up, thinking the town thinks that she killed herself."

"Do you think," I started, hesitating to finish my sentence. Veronica thumbed the cardboard flap of the box before she took it to Dee's desk and began packing up belongings. "Do you think she could've?" I finally asked.

Gingerly placing a picture frame into the box, Veronica only shrugged at my question, refusing to look away from the picture. "Could be," she said. Looking up at me she added, "I've known Dee my whole life—we're twins, did you know? Not identical, of course. She's two minutes older than me. I had breathing problems when I was born, crying made them worse. No matter what the doctors, nurses, or what my parents did, I wouldn't stop crying; they thought I'd die. It wasn't 'til they placed me besides Dee that I quieted down. There's this picture of her arm around me as newborns," Veronica smiled at the memory. "That's Dee, though, she was always there to help out."

I quietly began packing the math manipulatives stored behind the horseshoe table and Veronica talked. "She moved to Alton Oaks to help out our uncle—I still live in St. Louis, but I don't think she was ever going to move back. She was close to him—our uncle. Always was. He died last month and it hurt her. She really hasn't been the same—hasn't gotten over it. She asked Lyle to push back the wedding, but he had a cow, so they didn't." Veronica opened the top drawer of the desk and tentatively pulled out notebooks, opening them and seeing if they were to be packed. "Lyle won't admit that Dee was depressed about our uncle's passing, but I could tell it in our phone calls."

"I'm sorry you're going through all this. It's good that you and Lyle have each other for support," I added, taping the last box together.

Veronica made a non-committal sound and opened another drawer on Ms. Dempsey's desk. "I should've said something. A twin just knows, you know?"

I edged closer to the desk as a gesture of support and began taking the magnets and papers from the front of the desk and putting them in a box. "You're here now, right? That counts for something," I replied, hoping it did good.

Veronica sat back in the teacher's chair and took in the classroom. Packing it was going to be a big job. She sighed and ran her hand over the keyboard. Jake's words from our conversation last night replayed in my head: *There were no fingerprints on her keyboard. They had been wiped clean.* A chill shot down my back and I grabbed the corner of the desk to stand up.

"What is that?" I asked myself as I brushed reddish brown flakes from my hand.

Veronica's head peered over the desk as I inspected

the corner. "Is that," I gulped, "blood?"

CHAPTER NINE

The next morning I woke when the cool night air was still trapped in my bedroom, despite the sunshine outside. My eyes opened to my cell phone dancing on the bedside table. Afraid it was Jackson, I turned over and put a pillow over my head, muffling the sound the phone made when it hit the floor and continued to vibrate on the wooden planks beneath my bed.

I must have fallen asleep because the next thing I remembered, Sadie was jumping on my bed. The long, white chiffon shirt she wore barely hid the bathing suit she had on underneath, and her straw hat fell off as she jumped. "Wake up, Charli!" she chanted until she collapsed beside me. "Come on," she urged, pulling on my arm. "We're going boating!"

"*We* don't have a boat," I said, sitting up as I felt the heat of the day creeping into the room.

"No, but your brother does," she said, getting up and pulling open my dresser drawers.

"Alex has a boat? Since when?" I asked swinging my legs onto the floor.

Sadie pushed aside clothes until she found what she was looking for. "He's renting one. It's supposed to be ninety-two degrees today. And it's one of those rare Saturdays where we both don't have to work. Come on," she said, throwing my bathing suit at me. "You'll thank me later. It's a day of adventure!"

Twenty minutes later, I emerged from the bathroom wearing my bathing suit under a pair of cut-off jeans and black tank top that had *Las Vegas* bejeweled to the front. "Here's your hat and sunglasses!" Sadie said, springing up from her seat on the wicker hamper in the hallway.

She plopped the baseball cap on my head and stuck the sunglasses on my nose. "What? Did you ingest a pot of coffee for breakfast?" I asked, lazily following her down the hallway.

"Iced coffee and a chocolate croissant are waiting for you in the truck!" she replied enthusiastically and flew down the stairs. "Hopefully there's still ice in it."

As I stepped onto the front porch, the humidity was stifling. Sadie was already climbing into her red pick-up truck that was parked beside Mrs. Kratsky's golf cart.

"Leaving already?" my mother asked from the porch swing. She had a large pitcher of iced tea on the table where Jenna, Mrs. Kratsky, Bailey, and Carter—my brother-in-law—were sitting, fanning themselves in the early morning heat.

"It's supposed to be a hot one today," Mrs. Kratsky said, fanning herself with an intricate, colorful, Japanese fan.

"We're taking Eli to the cove in Mayfield today," Bailey said and turned to Carter and added, "as soon as the car is packed."

Carter smiled and raised his hands in defense. "I guess that's my cue to leave," he commented, and sashayed through the ladies on the porch.

Sadie honked her horn and leaned out of her window, "C'mon, Charli! Coffee and chocolate!" she yelled, jokingly reminding me of the treats that were awaiting me.

Climbing into her large truck was still a bit difficult since the wound I had gotten in my shoulder barely eight weeks ago wasn't completely healed yet. Alex had given me exercises to do as physical therapy, but I wasn't very good at keeping up with them.

Sadie watched me as I took a deep breath when I finally got into the truck. "Have you been doing your exercises?" she asked with a lifted eyebrow.

She had the air-conditioning on full blast and it hit the wisps of hair that weren't pulled back into a braid or by my cap. "Thanks for the coffee," I said, changing the subject, and took a sip.

"Honestly, Charli," she said, putting the car in reverse and pulling onto Oak Street, and sighed.

Unwrapping the chocolate croissant, I happily picked off bites as the radio played songs from the local country music station. As Sadie turned onto US-16, I asked, "Why are we driving anyway?" The boat rental and storage area were just on the other side of Gnarled Oaks Circle Drive, which would have been a twenty minute walk from the Alton house.

Stepping on the gas, we passed through the acres of oak trees. "Alex walked to the boat rental from your house this morning. We're going to meet him at the Sandbar in Sheridan."

"Why?" I asked.

Sadie shook her head. "Honestly, Charli, how did you survive without me in New Mexico?" I looked at her inquisitively as I swallowed the last of my chocolate croissant. "This is an epic Saturday. *EPIC.* It's the first Saturday you, Alex, and I can hang out together since you've been back. We're going to do it right. Which means you and I are going to lounge on the deck of the Sandbar, drinking mimosas, with our heads back, laughing in the sunshine, until our boat arrives for a day of epic fun."

I laughed, wondering how many times I was going to hear the word "epic" today. In good fun, I agreed to indulge Sadie in her "epic" day of fun.

So, forty minutes later, Sadie and I were

uncomfortably lounging on the hot-to-the-touch, weather-beaten deck of the Sandbar, sipping on weak mimosas from plastic cups, under an umbrella whose shade did not cover us. The Sandbar was a bar and restaurant on the Whett River in Sheridan that had a parking lot for both cars and boats. It was popular due to its access to the river, the fact that it served alcohol, and the live bands that played on the weekends.

"Is this how you pictured it?" I asked Sadie, placing my semi-cold drink against my sunburnt shoulders. The river was already crowded with boats. We watched tubers and jet skiers zoom by as we sipped our drinks.

Sadie tilted her head back and laughed dramatically. In an old Hollywood accent, where she didn't pronounce her R's, she replied, "Oh Cha'li, you ah cha'ming. Simply cha'ming, da'ling."

I laughed, despite burning alive in the sun. Alex pulled up in a twenty-five foot boat with a launchpad in the back. "Pip, pip!" Sadie exclaimed, continuing her accent and rising from her chair. "Adventu'e awaits, da'ling!"

Following her to the deck already lined with boats, we watched as Alex pulled the boat into an empty space, looping the rope around one of the poles to pull it in for a tight tie-up. "Your carriage," Alex said, taking Sadie's hand so she could board the boat on the bow, "awaits."

"Thank you, Alexande'," she said adjusting the large straw beach bag she had on her shoulder, once her sandaled feet were planted on the floor of the vessel. "Pleasant time in the country we had, isn't that so, Cha'li, da'ling?" she asked moving towards the back of the boat.

Alex helped me onto the boat and asked, "Is she going to talk like that the whole time?"

"I wouldn't doubt it," I responded, smiling.

Looking back, Sadie sat in one of the white vinyl seats in her straw hat, black sunglasses, and sipping the last of her mimosa. "Cheerio, all!" she said, waving at no one in particular and blew kisses into the wind. "Captain! To epic adventu'es!" she exclaimed, pointing down the river and then adjusted her chiffon cover-up.

Alex and I exchanged looks before we made preparations to leave the dock.

Twenty minutes up the river was a town called Sandlewood. It was a really hoity-toity town with million dollar mansions on the river and yachts parked at private docks. Just beyond the bend, the river widened and we decided to drop anchor near the shallows, where the weeds and cattails thrived, several yards from shore.

Plugging in Sadie's iPod, she and I took off our sandals and sat on the launch pad, soaking our feet in the river. Sadie held a bag of grapes that were no longer frozen, but still refreshingly cold. "Perfection," Sadie said with a sigh. "This is why I could never leave Alton Oaks." In the distance another boat dropped anchor and we could just hear Billy Joel streaming from their speakers.

Sadie offered me her bag of grapes. "I do miss this," I admitted, taking a handful. I still wasn't sure if I wanted to stay in Alton Oaks, but I was positive that Sadie was trying to sway me in a certain direction.

"Whoa!" I exclaimed with a sour face after I bit into a grape. "Did you soak these in—?"

Sadie shoved another grape in my mouth, put a finger to her lips and said, "Shh."

"Geronimo!" my brother yelled as he nearly jumped over us and cannonballed into the water. The resulting splash had both Sadie and me wiping off our sunglasses. When his head popped out of the water he yelled back, "You're welcome!"

Sadie playfully argued with him and tried to splash him back. Soon Sadie, too, was in the water.

I couldn't remember the last time I went swimming in the river and didn't realize how much I missed it: the thin cool blanket of water over your skin and the squishy mud beneath your toes and tickle of curious fish against your legs. Feeling the seaweed lazily scrape across your limbs and the occasional fish or turtle that would bump into you—it relaxes and energizes you at the same time. I wished I could jump in and join the both of them, but I couldn't risk infection to my shoulder wound.

Sipping on the coconut-flavored alcoholic beverage that Sadie referred to as her special "boat drink," I watched the families speeding down the river, often towing a screaming family member in a contraption behind them. The wake from each boat would eventually reach our vessel, making it sway slightly and the water lapped at the plastic I sat upon. The motion was like a lullaby and, mixed with Sadie's boat drink and booze soaked fruit, I was completely relaxed.

"Hey, neighbor." His voice was shockingly close and I opened my eyes to see Rip in a small, lime green, nine foot kayak a few feet in front of me.

"Hey," I greeted in surprise. "What are you doing out here?"

Rip extended the other end of his paddle to me. Raising his eyebrows and nodding his head, he said, "A little help?"

I grabbed the paddle and pulled him in sideways. He kept one hand on the launch pad so that he wouldn't drift away in the wake of the other boats. "Thanks," he said. "I was out kayaking down the stream there, in that outlet." He pointed past the cattails and I saw a small waterway that only a kayak would fit through.

"For fun?" I asked in disbelief.

With one hand he uncapped his water bottle and shrugged. "Yeah." Though he wore a life vest, he was shirtless beneath it and his skin had become extremely tan.

"Hey guys," Sadie said, swimming up alongside the kayak. Her auburn hair looked brown when it was wet and it made her blue eyes glow against the murky river water. Alex popped above water next to her a few seconds later.

"Hey," I said with a smile. "I'm not sure if you guys met, but this is Sadie, and my brother Alex," I introduced.

Sadie smiled and then climbed onto the launch pad, pulling her green towel around her. Automatically she put on her hat and sunglasses and reached for a bottle of sunblock. "Hey," Alex greeted, pulling himself onto the launch pad beside me. "You're Rip, right? Heard all about you." Alex pulled another towel from a nearby chair and started wiping off his head and shoulders. He was starting to get a tan, too.

"Still hard to get used to this small town stuff," Rip commented.

"You want to join us? We have plenty of room," Alex said, standing up. "It's adventure day," he commented. "Right, Sadie?" he called over his shoulder.

Sadie was taking a swig of her boat juice and gave him a thumbs up.

"No, thanks man," Rip said. "I'll just paddle back to Alton Oaks."

"But it's adventure day," I said to Rip.

"Yeah. It's no problem," Alex said, putting his white polo shirt on over his head. "We can tow the kayak, no biggie."

Rip looked from Alex to me and and while Alex rummaged through the cooler, I mouthed to Rip,

"Adventure day."

"Oh, fine," he said with an eye roll. "It won't hurt to be social for one day I guess," he added, grabbing the rope from the stern.

When the sun sunk low in the sky and our cooler was empty, we decided to dock at the Sandbar for a few burgers. Rip tied the bow to the deck and then ran to secure the stern as Alex sat in the cockpit. As Sadie and I precariously climbed out of the bow, the roaring music of an eighties cover band vibrated the metal deck. "Oh, I love this song!" Sadie exclaimed with too much emotion. She began dancing while I giggled uncontrollably.

"Come on, Sadie," Alex said, grabbing her elbow. "This way." He led her onto the grass and to a table close to the dance floor.

I followed barefoot, holding my flip-flops in my hand, feeling my eyes get misty from the amount of laughing I was doing. Rip came up behind me as I set foot in the grass. "Sadie isn't always like this, is she?" he asked, humored.

"You mean a wonderful human being? Yeah. Pretty much all the time," I responded, holding onto his shoulder as I put on my flip-flops. "Boat drinks magnify her awesomeness," I added.

With my sandals secure on my feet, Rip and I joined Sadie and Alex at the table they claimed. It was covered in empty plastic cups and baskets of cold, half-eaten appetizers. Immediately, a woman wearing tight, black shorts and a form-fitting orange tank top took our order of burgers and fries as she cleared the table.

"Can we eat on the boat?" Sadie asked like it was the greatest idea ever.

"No!" I protested. "Music!" I pointed out, tugging on her arm. "*Come on, Eileen!*" My feet were already dancing to the catchy 80's tune.

Sadie's face was animated with confusion. "I'm not Eileen," she said. "I'm Sadie."

I giggled a little too much at her response.

"Please, Alex?" Sadie asked, hilariously trying to stick out her bottom lip.

Alex sighed, hiding an amused smile, and looked at Rip. "I got her," Rip said, nodding his head towards me. "No worries."

"You got nothing," I said defensively and got up to dance as Alex and Sadie went back to the boat with their food.

Escaping Rip's grasp, I sashayed my way onto the dance floor. Near my spot by the lead guitarist as the band belted out Michael Jackson's "Beat It," I could just see Rip sipping his plastic cup of beer at the table. His gaze noncommittally swept across the patrons.

After dancing with a rotund man in leather and a white beard for a few songs, I plopped down next to Rip as he emptied his glass. Without much of a reaction, he slid my burger and fries in front of me and asked, "Are you ready to eat now?"

I should have felt offended for being treated like a toddler, but I was suddenly famished. Without an ounce of discretion, I took the largest bite I could muster out of the burger. I wiped away the ketchup that had gathered on my cheek as I chewed.

My head swimming in music, I rocked in my seat as I ate. Rip was looking at a map on his phone, seemingly not interested in keeping company.

"We're in Sandlewood just north of Alton Oaks," I informed and took another bite.

Rip pressed a button so the screen on his phone went black and he grunted. The entire chorus of Lionel Richie's "All Night Long" passed before I asked, "What are you looking for?"

"Nothing," Rip replied, shrugging. His eyes swept across mine briefly and then returned to the band.

I rolled my eyes. "It's very frustrating how evasive you are sometimes," I admitted, picking up part of the tomato that slipped out of my burger.

Rip sighed and raised his empty glass to the waitress, signaling a refill. "Don't worry about me," Rip remarked, stealing a fry from my basket. His plate held empty wax paper, no crumbs left of his food, not even a splotch of ketchup.

"Who said anything about worry?" I asked offended. "I'm just nosy."

Rip's lips pulled into a small smile as he ran his fingers around his empty cup, the crinkle of plastic as he squeezed it played on a nerve.

The band started playing Billy Idol's "Mony, Mony" as the waitress dropped off another beer for Rip. Swallowing the last bite of my burger, I studied Rip as he sat back in the plastic lawn chair. He slouched so that his knees stuck out further from his seat. One hand still grasped his phone, which sat in his lap; the black device stood out against his khaki shorts. The other hand loosely wrapped around the sweating plastic cup of beer and his gaze swept through the crowd on the dance floor. "Why did you move to Alton Oaks?" I asked, not sure why I did.

His hazel eyes met mine with a hint of amusement. "Why did *you*?" he asked, knowing full well that comment would stop our conversation.

Not wanting to deal with his evasiveness and get frustrated, I pushed away the fries left in my basket and popped out of my seat. "I'm done," I simply replied and walked back to the dock. I turned only once and saw Rip standing at the table, throwing down a bill, and emptied his cup in what seemed like one large gulp.

CHAPTER TEN

Sadie and I were sprawled out on the cushioned seats on the bow of the boat while the horizon smeared with streaks of red and orange and a few stars started popping up in the dark purple of the eastern sky. We were about to pull into the docks in Alton Oaks to return the boat and end our epic day of adventure. I basked in the cool late evening air as it hit our faces and our heads bobbed as we traveled over the wakes in the river.

While Alex returned the boat to the facility in Alton Oaks, we waited for him on the Canal Trail. Sadie was lying on the pavement and trying to get me to join her for star-gazing, pulling on my arm. "I don't think that's a good idea," Rip said, looking up and down the trail, just as I sat down. He had returned his kayak and beat Alex back to us on the path.

"Hush," Sadie said waving her hand.

Just then Alex pulled himself from the shadows and joined us under the well-lit path. He grabbed Sadie's hand with a good-humored smile. "Come on, Sadie," he urged, pulling her up. "Time to go home."

"But the stars!" she protested.

"We can star-gaze on the walk home," he recommended with a smile.

"I am so excited to walk home!" Sadie exclaimed, pulling on Alex's arm, finding her second wind.

"Can you make it?" Alex asked as Sadie leaned on him. I wondered if he'd thought through this plan.

"Of course I can!" Sadie declared. "A moonlight

stroll with my favorite person? No amount of boat drinks can keep me from that!" She turned to me and added, "No offense, Charli."

"None taken," I said.

"Make sure my sister gets home, will you?" Alex said over his shoulder to Rip.

He nodded and I watched Alex and Sadie walk west, towards downtown. Without saying a word, I started marching north, where I'd have to cross a patch of oak trees before running into Gnarled Circle Drive. "Hey, hold on," Rip interjected, grabbing my arm.

"Home this way," I said, pointing towards the trees.

"Yes, but motorcycle, this way." He pointed towards the parking lot.

"Okay. Bye then," I said bluntly and turned.

Again, Rip grabbed my arm. "I promised your brother I'd get you home and I will, but I'm not leaving my bike here."

Letting out an exaggerated sigh, I rolled my eyes. "But that means we have to go all the way to Sheridan and home is right over there," I pointed out and crossed my arms over my chest.

"Please?" Rip asked, the gold flecks in his eyes begged. "Come on. Epic adventure day, right?" When I did not give in, he pleaded, "Please don't make me leave my bike here. Please?"

Rolling my eyes I finally agreed.

There were only a few cars left in the parking lot and only one motorcycle. "What? No helmet?" I asked as he sat down on the bike. "I'm not getting on without a helmet. It's the law," I protested stubbornly.

Rip reached behind him and unlocked the storage compartment and pulled out a helmet. Happily, I stuck it on my head—it smelled brand new, like leather and chemicals, and I wondered if he ever used it. The tinted Plexiglas made my vision too dark and a small bout of panic set in. My slightly inebriated mind didn't think to take the helmet off. "Hold on," Rip said through a sigh, getting off the bike and grabbing my arm before I freaked out too much and fell over.

Raising the protective shield, the night air flooded into the helmet. "Better?" he asked, staring down at me with a hint of impatience I could tell he was trying to hide. I didn't answer and he sat back down on the bike. "Get on," he instructed as he fiddled with the controls on the console.

Hesitantly I draped my leg over the bike. "I don't think I should be doing this in my condition," I said, suddenly starting to feel dizzy.

"Just hold on tight," he said as the bike roared to life. "I'll get you home in no time."

We cruised through the empty streets of Sheridan with the wind rushing at our faces. When Rip merged onto US-16, he pulled the throttle and the air lashed at our cheeks. I wanted to close my eyes, but every time I did, I got dizzy. It was like being on an amusement park ride where I quietly hummed a melody so I wouldn't scream.

We passed the sign welcoming us to Alton Oaks and some time after we passed Blackhill Avenue, flashing red and blue lights lit up the trees around us. The wind carried Rip's string of swear words to my ears as he slowed the bike and pulled to the side of the highway.

"Of course," Rip said vehemently, more to himself than to me. I let go of my death grip on Rip and leaned back, trying to figure out what the problem was.

"Mr. Oakley." The police officer said his name in a high-hat way. When I lifted my head to see the officer past the helmet, I was surprised to see Jake. "And Charli?" he asked, dumbfounded.

"Hi, Jake," I said, smiling.

"What are you doing?" he asked, the stoic cloak of

the deputy's authority momentarily absent from his tone.

"Apparently keeping a promise to my brother," I shared, still not liking the idea of taking the motorcycle home rather than walking. I then tried to take the helmet off my head, struggling with it as Jake and Rip continued their conversation.

"Do you know why I pulled you over, Mr. Oakley?" Jake asked with his hand on his belt.

"I can only guess what your excuse is this time," Rip said sardonically with an eye roll.

"You were traveling five miles over the speed limit," Jake informed.

Rip ran a hand through his hair. "Sure. Right. Can we make this a warning so I can get her home?" Rip asked, pointing his thumb over his shoulder at me.

I continued to struggle with getting the helmet off.

"And you're operating a motorcycle on the highway without a helmet," Jake paused for a moment and added, "and is that alcohol I smell on your breath?"

"Oh, come on," Rip protested. "You've just been waiting to get me on something. This is profiling!"

"I'm going to have to ask you to step away from the vehicle, sir," Jake said backing away.

"You can't be serious," Rip remarked agitatedly.

"Come on," Jake said matter-of-factly. "I need you to walk the line."

"This is ridiculous," Rip mumbled, getting off the bike.

As they bickered on the side of the road, I got off the bike and tugged at the helmet. I stumbled into the tall grass and weeds, feeling dizzy with each tug.

"Finally!" I said when it popped off, feeling the cool night air wipe away the sweat around my hairline. Taking a moment to get my bearings, I grabbed the steel bar of the roadway speed limit sign and then peppered the tall weeds with the burgers and fries I had had for dinner onto the side of the road.

CHAPTER ELEVEN

The sun rose angrily on Sunday, evaporating any tendrils of cool night air that dared to linger. It was too hot to stay in bed, even with the box fan whirring in exertion from my bedroom window. Heavy-footed and nursing a headache, I grabbed a glass of water and walked to the porch swing, hoping I could catch a short nap in the cooler air while Mom and Dad ate breakfast in the kitchen. It wasn't long before I heard heavy-soled shoes climbing the porch stairs.

With one arm draped over my forehead to block out the menacing light, I managed to open one eye. Jake was approaching the front door until he noticed me lying on the swing. I sat up as his feet made too much noise traveling across the porch. "You've been teaching only three days and already you've gone wild," he remarked, handing me a to-go cup from The Buzz.

Not finding the humor in his words, I only grunted and reached for the cup. My eyes were too tired to open fully and I squinted in the morning light. "To or from work?" I asked, noticing he was in his uniform.

"From," he replied, sitting down on the wooden bench. "After I brought you home and impounded Rip's bike—"

"You impounded his bike?" I asked aghast.

"Yeah," he said with a hint of righteousness.

I took a long sip of coffee, letting it disintegrate the sleepy veil from my eyes. "What is wrong with you two?" I asked, putting a hand to my forehead, wishing I had a pair of sunglasses to tone down the sun.

Jake ignored my comment and continued, "When I stopped Rip last night I was on my way back from Sandlewood where Ms. Dempsey's autopsy had taken place."

Savoring another long sip of coffee, my brain finally started to climb out of the fog. "And?" I asked, leaning in and hoping he would share what he knew.

Jake bit his lip and replied, "Remember what I told you? That I didn't think it was suicide?"

I nodded, not taking my eyes from him. I hoped that as long as I was looking at him, he'd keep talking.

"I was right," he admitted barely above a whisper. Shock left my mouth ajar. "There was a head wound prior to death." He paused for a moment as if he struggled to divulge more information. "It was murder," he confided.

"Murder?!" My mother's voice shot out of the living room window from behind the sheer curtains that faintly billowed in a cross-breeze. She was eavesdropping again.

Jake winced and regret covered his features.

"Mom!" I scolded too forcefully through the window. It took a lot to get Jake to share these details with me and now I was sure he would never tell me anything again.

As the heat ate away at the morning, I found my spot on the front porch extremely comfortable and hogged it as the sun slipped across the roof and into the front yard. For a moment in the early afternoon, I wedged my way into the stifling house to pour a glass of lemonade. When I returned to the front porch, Mrs. Kratsky was coming down Oak in her golf cart with my mother in the passenger seat.

Sinking into the porch swing, gripping the sweating glass of lemonade, I watched as the two women exited the golf cart and began climbing up the creaking stairs. Both were dressed in funeral clothes and the dark colors, mixed with the heat of the day, made both of their faces glisten. Immediately, I went back into the kitchen and fetched the pitcher of lemonade with two additional glasses.

"Oh Charli, you're a saint," my mother exclaimed as she plopped on the porch swing. The chains above rattled with her sudden weight.

Mrs. Kratsky eagerly gulped half her glass before sharing, "It's been a helluva day today."

"Where are you two coming from? A funeral?" I asked, half joking.

Mom nodded. "We went to Terryville to pay our respects to Ms. Dempsey." Terryville had the closest funeral home to us, but some Alton Oaks residents preferred to hold funerals in their homes, like the generations before them. Apparently this wasn't the case for Ms. Dempsey.

Mrs. Kratsky swayed back and forth in the rocking chair and wisps of her hair rustled in the airy movement. "There were so many students there, you wouldn't believe it," she commented.

"I would think so, considering how well liked she was among them," I said, suddenly wondering if I should have made an appearance.

Just then a red Nissan kicked up the dust on Oak as it moved east and pulled into Jenna's driveway. My cousin, her husband Mark, and my sister all climbed out of the car also dressed in black. I watched as Mark waved to the women and walked into the house, probably looking for a reprieve from the heat. Both Jenna and Bailey had air-conditioning in their updated houses.

In their coal black heels, they crossed the grass with grace until they reached my mother's front porch.

"Mother," said Bailey in a chastising tone, as she reached the top of the stairs. "You didn't have to take the tri-city bus to Sandlewood. You both could have driven with us. Or I could have let you borrow our car." Happily, I gave up my seat on the porch swing to Bailey as I went inside to refill the pitcher of lemonade.

When the springs of the screen door screeched to signal my return, no one seemed to notice. They were already gossiping about what they saw at the funeral. "Oh, her skirt was much too short!" Mrs. Kratsky said, shaking her head and pulling out her colorful Japanese-inspired paper fan from her purse. "I mean it was her sister's own funeral. What a sign of disrespect," she added, beginning to fan herself.

I placed the tray I was carrying onto the table and began pouring Jenna and Bailey each a glass of lemonade. "I don't know," Bailey said, taking the cold glass from me. "She probably didn't mean disrespect. It's a different time, and it's a hot day."

"And, at the risk of sounding arrogant," Jenna added, "her sister didn't seem like the conservative type. She probably didn't realize it would upset people, knowing that she comes from a..." She paused for a moment to lower her voice in a scandalous tone, "different background."

I sat down on the ledge, feeling a little out of place in my old volleyball shorts and ratty white tank top that I hadn't the energy to change out of yet. "What do you mean by 'different background?' She seemed perfectly normal to me," I shared, feeling the slightest hint of a breeze that didn't completely erase the sweat on the back of my neck.

"You met her?" my mother asked, staring me down.

I winced, realizing that my mother took my lack of gossip as an insult to her. "Only briefly," I said in defense. "After school on Friday. I was helping pack up

Ms. Dempsey's room and she walked in with the fiancé."

My mother bit her lip and her look said *We'll talk later*. I looked at Jenna, hoping that she'd answer my question.

Jenna shifted uncomfortably in her seat, tugging at the hem of her ash-black dress. "She doesn't seem well educated," she said.

I lifted an eyebrow.

"She's from St. Louis, the inner city," Jenna added. "I overheard someone at the funeral say she's a janitor, that she lives with five roommates."

"Maybe that's all she can afford as a janitor," I said, taking some offense to what Jenna was implying.

Bailey's pastel green finger nails picked at her black lace skirt as she added, "But the five roommates..." She trailed off in disenchantment without looking up from her knee.

Mrs. Kratsky shook her head and tisked. Mom silently poured herself another glass of lemonade. "What? Is that code for something?" I asked, my tone bordering on incredulousness.

"Charli," my sister said in a hushed key, briefly meeting my gaze. "Everyone knows when you live in the inner city and have that many roommates, it's a drug den."

It took a lot of energy not to immediately respond to this accusation without causing a lot of friction. First of all, I know how expensive it is to live in a city. Secondly, I knew a lot of people who joined service positions after the Peace Corps and lived with a number of roommates (sometimes in tents in the backyard!) just to follow their passion. And, lastly, how dare they jump to that accusation!

Tactfully, after counting to five in my head, I said, "That's automatically believing the worst in somebody.

Besides wearing a short skirt and living in St. Louis, what makes you think she lives in a drug den?"

"I overheard her talking about traveling out of the country. She said she had been to Honduras and Nicaragua a few times and frequents the Dominican Republic," my sister divulged as if this information certified every rumor percolating on the porch this afternoon. My eyes swept across the other occupants, hoping someone saw my side, but everyone avoided my gaze, with a look that said they knew better: poor, naïve, Charli.

"And I spent two years in some of the most deprived parts of Costa Rica. Does that make me a drug addict?" I asked defensively, feeling my blood pressure go up.

"We're not saying she's a drug addict necessarily," my sister said in a voice my mother used to use when we were hysterical as children, "but maybe a drug mule."

Crossing my arms over my chest, I rolled my eyes. Their small town minds were infuriating sometimes.

"Let's not get hung up on this topic," my mother said. "Charli, dear, would you mind refilling the pitcher?" she asked, picking up the nearly empty glass container. What was left of the ice cubes, swirled around the bottom, hit the sides, and clinked. I knew what she was doing; she was trying to put Bailey and me in separate corners to cool down.

Grabbing the pitcher a little too forcefully, I disappeared into the stifling house, wondering if Alton Oaks was really where I belonged.

Banging the glass pitcher onto the kitchen counter, little droplets of water hit my arm and shirt and I let out a frustrated sigh, more so because Bailey got to stay on the porch and I was temporarily banished into the house.

Pulling the canister of powered lemonade mix from

the cabinet, I let it crash nosily onto the counter. Placing the pitcher into the sink basin, I let the cold water collect while I tried to squash a torrential storm of emotions that threatened to break loose.

Turning off the faucet, I put both my hands on the counter and leaned against it, taking a few deep breaths as perspiration gathered on my upper lip. Why was I getting so upset? Dealing with Bailey was something I thought I had mastered by now.

Who was I kidding? It wasn't Bailey. It was the fact that, two months after I left Jackson I was still living with my parents, lost. I had no clue where to go from here. Sure, I had gotten a job at the elementary school, but was going back to teaching what I really wanted? Especially if someone as amazing as Ms. Dempsey wasn't doing enough to please the administration?

And what about Jackson? Why couldn't I make up my mind on how to handle him? Why was the idea of him still causing so much pain? Why was it such a hazy gray area that I couldn't even think straight when it came to him?

Wiping the few tears that had rolled down my cheeks, I told myself now was not the time for a breakdown. I was stronger than that. Opening the freezer for the ice cube tray, I lingered, letting the icy blast wipe away the perspiration gathering on my face. Closing my eyes, I counted to ten and inhaled the freezer-burned smell of French fries, forcing myself to cool down.

Carrying the heavy pitcher out of the kitchen, I hesitated before opening the screen door, hearing hushed tones. "She had a rough night; don't take offense to it," my mother said.

"Rough!" my sister exclaimed a little too loudly for their clandestine conversation. "Is it true she stole that guy—Rip's?—motorcycle in a drunken escapade and then threw up all over the Alton Oaks police force?"

My mouth fell open at how twisted some rumors in this town could become.

"No!" my mom exclaimed. "Rip was giving her a ride home and—lord, I do not trust that guy—he ended up getting pulled over. Jake gave her a ride home. That's it."

"I think there are more colors to that story that you're leaving out," my sister said coldly.

My mother stumbled over words. I realized she was trying to change the subject and warmth for her filled my heart. "Did you know Ms. Dempsey was murdered?" she spat out.

I forcefully swung open the screen door and chastised my mother. "Mom!" All heads turned to me and some of the lemonade spilled over the lip of the pitcher as I walked. My poor mother looked like Bailey did in high school when my dad would catch her tip-toeing across the threshold, long past her curfew.

I placed the pitcher back on the table, letting the ice cubes slosh a few drops over the edge. Standing between Mrs. Kratsky and Jenna, and across from my mother and Bailey, I put my hands on my hips and stared my mother down. "I mean, we think she was, right?" my mother added unconvincingly.

The women looked between my mother and me, confused. Finally, before anyone could inquire further about my mother's accusation, Mom had added, "Oh! Remember the man with the rose at the funeral? Who was he?"

The question seemed to snap everyone out of their confused stupor and Jenna reported, "Oh, yeah. That was the janitor at the elementary school. William or Raymond or Albert? I don't remember his name."

"Walter," I said, going back to leaning on the ledge, arms crossed. "His name is Walter."

Bailey ignored me and asked, "He seemed a little too emotional. And what was with the rose?"

"To be fair," Mrs. Kratsky said, giving me a nod, "It's a social obligation to give flowers at funerals."

A small grin played at the corners of my mouth and I wanted to give her a hug for trying to not jump to conclusions.

Bailey looked to Jenna for encouragement. "You can't tell me there was nothing more to it than a social obligation. He was really upset."

Jenna shrugged. "I didn't notice. I was too busy trying to figure out what was going on between Dee's fiancé and the principal."

"Ohh," Bailey sang with interest, her elbow on her knees and leaning forward. Small wisps of hair near her ears had fallen from the bun on the top of her head and danced with the movement. "What happened?"

"Nothing too dramatic," Jenna said and took a sip of her lemonade. Her fingers played at the rim of her glass as she continued. "I went to give my condolences to Dee's fiancé and I shared with him how much good she has done for those kids and Principal Newton snuffed. Lyle—the fiancé—his face got red and Dee's sister escorted the principal out of the viewing room with enough finesse that not many people noticed."

"That principal seems a bit," my mother appeared to think about the right word to use and said, "rigid." She looked from Jenna and me, expecting confirmation.

Jenna waved her hand and the silver bangle bracelets clanked as they slid up and down her hand. "She's a bit austere, but she does it for the good of the school. We went from a D-ranking school to an A+ school within two years of her being the principal. She even revisited the budget, finding funding to purchase new textbooks. It's nice to have history books that don't refer to Russia as the U.S.S.R. anymore."

I put the lip of my glass to my lips and sipped the cold liquid slowly, letting the ice cubes numb my lip, so I wouldn't go on another rant about schools and administration.

The porch grew quiet, not even the birds were chirping out in this heat. The floorboards creaked along with the rocking chair and the ice in our drinks splashed as we drank. "So," Mrs. Kratsky said, breaking the silence. "Another murder, huh? I don't know if I should be happy it wasn't suicide, or upset that Alton Oaks has another murder."

I winced; I knew we had wandered off that topic way too easily. My mother caught my eye with a hint of panic. "Hypothetically, of course," I clarified.

"I mean, we can't say for sure it was murder; we're not the police," my mother added, busying herself by topping off everyone's glasses.

"Murder would make more sense," Jenna said. "Dee seemed to love teaching too much. She was always smiling. Always so happy. And she was getting married in two weeks." Jenna suddenly turned somber. "Oh! Poor, Lyle. He has to go and cancel all the wedding plans and deal with Dee's death. That poor man."

"Well, if it *is* murder, who do you think killed her?" Bailey asked, turning to my mother.

My mother thought about it and then put down her glass. "It would have to be somebody who had access to the school. Someone who knew her, obviously. Someone who took the time to stage a suicide instead of leaving a murder scene."

"And," Mrs. Kratsky interjected, "someone who had an issue with her. Maybe wanted her out of the picture. Maybe someone who would benefit from her death or her absence."

"Lyle!" my sister exclaimed.

All heads turned to her, some with interest and some

in confusion. "What? How?" I asked incredulously.

Looking at me, Bailey pursed her lips together and straightened her shoulders. Turning to the group she said, counting on her fingers, "He had access to the school. He obviously knew her more than anyone, and he was certainly strong enough to hoist her up onto the beam."

"But why?" my mother asked.

Bailey bit her lip. "Not sure yet," she admitted. "Maybe jealousy?"

"Jealousy?" my mother asked, lifting an eyebrow and playing with the pendant on her necklace.

"Oh, I don't know," Bailey said, slightly upset. Perhaps she hadn't thought out her accusation before she said it.

"What about a student?" Mrs. Kratsky asked.

"A student?" Jenna asked, tilting her head. Her blonde hair fell over her shoulder and brushed her chin. "They're kids."

"A past student then?"

"She had only been teaching in Alton Oaks a few years. Her oldest students would be in ninth grade by now," Jenna reported.

Mrs. Kratsky scrunched up her nose and said, "Well, I guess not a student then."

My mother then gasped as if a bee had just stung her. "The janitor! Wallace!" she said.

"Walter," I corrected.

"Walter," my mother said, glancing in my direction. "He has access to the school, knows her, and was extremely upset at the funeral."

"Maybe he was upset because he was guilt-ridden. Haunted by the memories of killing her!" my sister dramatically added.

"But why?" Jenna asked as if this was a possibility.

Mom's shoulders slumped. "I don't know."

"Well, this is getting us nowhere," Mrs. Kratsky said getting up from the rocking chair, her knees clicking with age. "Maybe it really was a suicide."

No one on the porch agreed, but no one disagreed either.

"I'm heading home to get out of these clothes. They're cramping my style," she added and stepped away from the rocker. "Stay cool, spring chickens," she added with a wink and a wave.

I smiled at her. Sometimes she was like a teenager trapped in an eighty-year old's body.

"I should go too. I have five IEP meetings tomorrow, back-and-forth between the schools. It's going to be a long day," Jenna admitted, rising from the bench.

Bailey followed suit. "If you want a break from the heat, you can hang out in our air-conditioning for a while," she said to our mother.

"Thanks, Bailey," she smiled. "Maybe. I'll see you for dinner tonight, eight o'clock."

Bailey smiled and, ignoring me, made a beeline to her house, crossing from shady patch of grass to shady patch of grass until she reached her front steps.

"Charli," my mom said with sorrow brushing the lines around her eyes. "It breaks my heart when you and your sister butt heads like that. You're the older—"

I cut her off, suppressing an eye roll, "The older sister. I should know better. I know, I know." Boy, I did not miss this undying conversation while living in Albuquerque.

Mom swallowed her words and stood. A line of sweat appeared on her dark gray turtleneck. "I'm going to take a shower. Be ready by seven-fifteen. We're having dinner at Oakie's with the family," she instructed

"The family?" I asked.

Mom turned and nodded. "You, me, Dad, Bailey, Carter, and Eli."

The eight year old in me wanted to stomp my foot and whine. "No Alex?" I asked, searching for a glimmer of hope.

Shaking her head and opening the screen door she reported, "No, he's working."

I fell onto the porch swing, the chains clanking, and draped an arm across my eyes after Mom walked inside. Groaning, I beckoned for a large bout of patience, or a creative excuse to get out of a family dinner sure to be full of tension and frustration, at least on my part.

CHAPTER TWELVE

When Mom returned to the front porch after her shower, her short blonde hair still wrapped in a baby blue towel, I had a long, exhausting talk with her about confidentiality and not eavesdropping on my conversations. Then, as she started asking questions about Jackson, I managed to escape to the backyard where I had a long, refreshing nap in the shaded hammock between the oaks. I managed to find an inner peace despite the fact that I was expected (not asked to) attend a family dinner at Oakie's. Somehow Dad found the opportunity early in the day to go and find work at Oakie's on his day off, and I was slightly jealous of him.

Mom and I slowly made our way down Oak Street just as the sun began its descent, hitting us square in the face. We walked along the north side of the street where there was more shade, but no sidewalk. Dust soon caked our feet and pebbles kept getting stuck in my sandals; Mom was the smart one who wore gym shoes and tried to hide her frustration at my slow pace. We were both relieved when we passed the cemetery and reached Sheridan Avenue, where the sidewalk appeared. The cement was so hot from the day's pummeling sun that I could feel it through my flip-flops.

As we cut behind the stores on the north side of east Main Street, we noticed a woman sitting on a bench near the parking lot, under the shade of the inn's blue awning. Her long dark hair draped in front of her face and her shoulders were slumped in defeat.

Her voice rose as we noticed she was talking into a cell phone and her body language bounced from anger to grief. She held something white in her other hand that was much too large to be a tissue or a handkerchief, but she kept pressing it to her tear-filled face. "Isn't that Ms. Dempsey's sister?" I asked, nudging my mother.

"Yeah. That's Veronica," my mom said with a sigh. The woman was still dressed in a deep violet dress—it reminded me of the color of the night sky, somewhere between the deepest night and the fainted glimmer of dawn. Her long legs were crossed and the hem of her skirt was scandalously high above her knee.

"Well, that's not what she told me!" we could hear her say before she hung up the phone and buried her face in the white cloth.

I veered to the left and Mom asked, "What are you doing?"

"Helping," I responded and Mom hesitated to follow. "She looks like she needs a friend."

I felt the dying rays of the sun still beat upon my skin and was thankful I had grabbed one of my dad's baseball caps before I left the house. "Are you okay?" I asked tentatively, standing beside the bench.

Veronica looked up from the balled up cloth in her hands. "Oh, yeah," she said unconvincingly, wiping her eyes with what I could now see was a t-shirt. "Lawyers," she added with a sniffle. The little mascara that still haunted her golden brown eyes was spotty and collected in the hint of premature wrinkles. "It's frustrating. I just can't wait to be done with this tragedy."

My mother appeared by my side. "I'm sorry to hear about your sister's murder," Mom said, her hands in the pockets of her denim skort. I sucked in a sharp breath through my teeth at my mother's blunt comment.

"Murder?" Veronica asked and looked up at the both of us confused. Her eyes were bloodshot and her cheeks were pink where her makeup had rubbed off.

"Yeah," Mom said sadly, looking at her dust-covered gym shoes. "Turns out she had head trauma before she was hung; didn't you hear?"

I poked my mother in the ribs, appalled by her nonchalantness, and shot her an angry look. Realizing her mistake, she discreetly backed away as Veronica looked back and forth between us.

"I," Veronica started, nearly speechless. "I have to go," she said clearly upset and darted from the bench, balling up the t-shirt she held in one hand.

"Mother," I scolded, approaching her, "Jake is going to kill you. You have to stop letting that slip."

Not wanting to be chastised by her daughter, and the heat of the day clawing at her patience, she sighed and said, "Let's just go," and marched ahead towards Oakie's.

Immediately after walking through the air-conditioned threshold of Oakie's Bar & Grill, we saw Bailey, Carter, and Eli already sitting at a table, just beyond the hostess' podium. Bailey, naturally, had Eli sitting in a booster seat at the foot of the table while Carter and she sat on either side. Eagerly, I grabbed the chair next to Carter, relieved that Mom had already pulled out the chair next to Bailey and slung the strap of her purse over the back. They were already talking about what had happened minutes ago in the inn's parking lot.

We had ordered and Dad arrived with the potato skins and salsa appetizers. Since he wasn't officially on the clock today, he wore a polo shirt instead of his dress shirt and tie. There was a small splattering of something on his shirt, near the belt, but it wasn't anything dramatic. He smiled at me with a wink as he purposely sat the salsa and chips in front of me.

"Hello, Charlotte May I," he said, kissing the top of my head and addressing me by my childhood nickname. He then made his rounds, greeting everyone at the table. I could tell he hesitated to sit down; he was always up and moving, that was natural for him.

He finally sat when our entrees came. Bailey and Mom gossiped, their heads together, unless Bailey turned to tend to Eli who was happily eating his plate of chicken nuggets. Carter and my father talked about Carter's job as a fireman, while I sat and ate my pulled pork sandwich, wishing Alex was there.

"Hey, Charli," Carter interrupted after swallowing a forkful of meatloaf. "Are you free next Saturday?" he asked.

I was always free. Nevertheless, I pretended to think about my calendar. "I think so. Why?"

"It's the Fireman's Charity Ball next Saturday. Do you want to babysit Eli?" he asked. He hid a wince as his leg jumped. By the look in Bailey's eyes, I assumed she had kicked him.

"Me?" I asked, unsure. I looked over at Eli who was pretending his French fries were planes and they were kamikazing into a puddle of ketchup. He was utterly content in his own little world.

"There's no pressure," Carter added, taking another bite of his meal. "If you don't want to, my parents will. I just thought that since you're back in town, you might want to spend time with your nephew."

"You trust me?" I asked.

He laughed. "Yeah, why not?"

I licked my lips, still weighing the question. "Has Bailey told you about her childhood? As my little sister?"

He looked at me questioningly.

"Okay, well, like, this one time when I was eight, I put Bailey—my four-year-old sister—in the front basket of my bike, which still had training wheels. I thought I was being an awesome big sister, but Mom thought otherwise."

"So did I!" Bailey chimed in. "Especially after I fell out and cut my forehead on the old fence post." She lifted her bangs and pointed to the scar.

Carter laughed. "Well, maybe we'll put Eli to sleep before we leave, so you don't have to interact with him that much."

I laughed with him. "Isn't that like the equivalent to training wheels when it comes to babysitting?" I asked.

"Mom will watch him, right?" Bailey said looking to her right.

Mom hesitated, her eyes flashing between my sister and me, before saying, "Yeah, of course. We'll always be there for Eli. But I'm sure Char—"

"Great! See?" Bailey exclaimed, cutting off Mom in mid-sentence. She turned to Eli and said, "Grandma gets to watch you! Yay!"

Eli cheered and then tried to make plans that involved popcorn, macaroni and cheese, and an army of X-men while my mother nodded enthusiastically.

With my appetite suddenly gone, I excused myself from the table, though no one really noticed. Originally, I planned to head towards the bathroom to escape my sister, but I made a sudden turn and walked out into the muted heat of Main Street. It was the hushed version of the day where the sunlight hovered, not ready to say good night, and the flies were loud and abundant.

Across the street, outside the post office, Veronica sat on the curb. She had changed out of her dress and into a plain black tank top and dark blue shorts. Her black hi-top sneakers added to the dark cloud of grief that hovered over her. I know how heavy that cloud could be, and no one should have to bear that storm alone.

Without a word, I sat down beside her. She still clung to the white t-shirt. When she looked up, I noticed that she had reapplied her eye makeup since I had seen her outside the inn. The eye shadow darkened her eyes and her mascara left clawing marks on her eyelids. "Do you want to talk about it?" I asked.

Veronica tried to answer, but started crying again and buried her face into the mascara-stained t-shirt. Putting a hand on her shoulder, I waited patiently and watched the line outside Froz T's grow.

The sun hovered above the horizon somewhere behind the stores and trees across the street. Veronica finally lifted her face from the cloth. "Charli, right?" she asked, her voice drenched in tears.

I nodded.

"Do you have a sister, Charli?"

Again, I nodded. "Yes."

"Can you imagine losing her?" she asked, choking on a wave of grief. "This," she said, a hand on her heart, "it hurts too much."

I thought about losing Bailey. We didn't always get along, especially today, but I'm sure it would hurt to lose her; to lose the memories we had yet to make. To see Eli grow up without a mother and Carter without the woman he had loved since sixth grade.

"Dee was the one with a good head on her shoulders. The rational one," Veronica shared, running a finger under each eye with the t-shirt. "I work on cruise ships down in Florida. I love the adventure and the lack of responsibility. I always put myself and my wants first. Dee wasn't that way. She didn't deserve..." Veronica trailed off and began crying once more.

"I don't know what I'm going to do without her. She was always there for me," Veronica shared in between tears. She clutched her chest in pain. "It's never going to stop," she said. "This pain, this guilt..."

Unsure how to help her with her grief, I said, "It might not stop, but it will get smaller." I took a deep breath, watching two bicyclists pedal down Main Street with their flashing safety lights. "One day you'll be able to pack it away and live with it. Once in a while it will be that pebble in your shoe that you can't ignore, but I don't think you'll ever want to. It reminds you that you're human. It will remind you of her."

After several moments, Veronica forced a pathetic smile at my attempt to help. It faded quickly and a hard somber look soaked her features. "I hope you *never* understand what I'm feeling, Charli," she said, her sharp stare nearly cutting a hole through the top of her shoe. When she looked up again her face softened a bit, "Thanks for listening, Charli."

CHAPTER THIRTEEN

The hallways before school on a Monday morning are almost as quiet as a mortuary on a slow day. Teachers lumber into the faculty lounge, hugging their empty mugs, hoping someone has already made a pot of coffee and that it was hot and strong. This Monday I was half asleep, already finishing the iced coffee I had made for the commute, as I walked through the door. Brittany wasn't behind the desk yet and the front office was too quiet, even for a Monday morning. Every other morning when I'd walked into the front office, there would be phones ringing, the metal clang of file drawers opening and closing, and the copier in the corner would hum as it spit out copies into a tray, permeating the air with the scent of melted plastic.

My eyes reluctantly swept past Principal Newton's office door and I hoped I wouldn't make eye contact. To my relief, the old knicked wooden door was closed, but I noticed the artificial light escaping from beneath it as I tripped over the gray nondescript carpet, so I knew she was already on campus, which was why I tip-toed past.

After signing in with the pink flower-tipped pen, I went on the hunt for more caffeine. As I rounded the corner of the *We Are Alton Oaks* mural that my mother's graduating class had painted in 1975, there were voices traveling down the hall that were much too animated for a Monday morning.

Two teachers stood outside the faculty room looking down the hallway and, due to the volume of voices, I guessed that many more teachers were inside the room. As I approached them, I realized what the hubbub was about: the door at the end of the hallway—the janitor's closet-slash-office—was covered in red drippy paint, and it spelled out the word MURDERER.

Apparently my mother's slip of the tongue traveled fast across the town. Suppressing a sigh, I looked down at my closed-toed, employee-handbook-approved footwear; I did not look forward to my next run-in with Jake. My fingers slid across the indent of the cell phone in the back pocket of my capris and wondered if Jake had already tried to contact me. Before I could slip my phone out and check, the door to the closet creaked opened, momentarily erasing any evidence of the graffiti, and Walter stepped out carrying a bucket and scrub brush.

"Did he kill her?" one of the teachers whispered, her brown curls brushing across her mustard yellow cardigan as she turned to her companion.

"Who painted that?" another teacher murmured, grasping her bulbous, yellow smiley face mug as she raised it to her lips.

Squeezing past the two women, I marched down the hallway and stood beside Walter who always seemed to be wearing the same outfit: jeans and a long-sleeve white cotton shirt. A patch of his gray hair comb-over fell out of place and brushed against his wire-rimmed glasses as he looked over at me quizzically.

"I haven't had a chance to introduce myself," I said, suddenly realizing that it might not have been the best time to do so, but brushed the notion away. "I'm Charli Parker. I just started."

His extremely gray and white bushy eyebrows dipped. "Yeah," he said nearly cutting me off. His jaw moved as if he was biting his tongue. "Yer the one who found her, didn'tcha?"

I nodded and picked up the rag that was draped over the side of the bucket. Starting to help him wipe off the paint, I nearly whispered, "Yes. I did."

For a few moments we worked in silence, methodically scrubbing the paint from the door. Inaudible whispers carried down the hallway and mixed with the sloshing of water as I rinsed the rag in the warm sudsy water. Some of the paint was still fresh and came off easily. "I didn't do it," Walter admitted over the sound of the bristles scraping against the wooden door. There were no longer voices coming from behind us, but I didn't dare turn around to check and see if the teachers were still there. "Did you ever meet 'er?" he asked.

"No," I said, shaking my head. "Unfortunately I didn't."

He scrubbed the last two letters of the graffiti off the door, but there was still a red hue where they once stood. "She was one of the nicest people I ever met," he said, still watching his hand move the scrub brush systematically over the graffiti. "I would never 'urt 'er," he informed. Creases of pain appeared around his eyes as he continued, "She was a friend. Always said hello. Made me cookies. Remembered my birthday."

He then stopped scrubbing. Turning to me with a look of confusion and despair he admitted, "It was my rope—a rope we use in the gym for displays and stage curtains. And I was gonna put 'em up for Heritage Night. It was from this 'ere closet, but I didn't give it to her, I didn't do it. Don't believe what they say, Charli Parker."

I bit my lip and felt the water from the rag drip down my arm. "Was she acting odd that day? Did you think anything was wrong?" I asked, wringing the rag out over the bucket.

Walter went back to scrubbing. "No," he admitted.

His gray and white mustache twitched. "Was a normal day. I did my rounds of vacuumin' and changin' the garbage liners 'round four. Ms. Dempsey was always my last classroom and she'd always have a chat with me. She would stay late nearly every day."

I made a mental note to see if Jake would let me know Ms. Dempsey's time of death. "What time do you think that was? When you last saw her?"

Walter rinsed out the scrub brush in the bucket as he replied, "I always get to her room 'bout five-thirty. We talked about the end of the summer an 'er weddin' that was comin' up sooner than she could believe. Not once did I think she was troubled. Not a once."

Shaking his head, Walter took a minute to sort out his feelings before he continued, "But I was in the gym 'til 'bout 6:30 setting up chairs and tables for Heritage Night. Never heard nothing. Never saw 'er leave neither, 'cause she'd always use the door in 'er room. I left campus 'round quarter-to seven. Was home in time to watch *Lincoln's Challenges*." Walter stopped scrubbing and looked down at his slip-resistant black shoes and said, "Oh! What if she was strugglin' and I was busy watchin' my favorite show?" His face grew white. "What if she died while I was setting up chairs, whistling away like a happy badger?"

I pitied him. Bailey was right when she said he looked pretty upset at the funeral. He had a lot of respect for Ms. Dempsey and he was obviously wondering if he couldn't have done something different to prevent it... as well as now dealing with murderer accusations.

"I'm sure she knew you were a friend. If she was in any trouble I'm sure she would have asked for your help," I said. "Try to take comfort in the fact that you were friends, and sometimes friendship is a bigger gift than you know."

"What is going on?!" Principal Newton's voice sliced through the otherwise silent hallway. I jumped like I was getting caught stealing.

The women in the faculty room scattered like roaches as Principal Newton's shoes *clack-clacked* across the hall. "Ms. Parker, it's eight o'clock. You're supposed to be on playground duty. Today's schedule is in your mailbox. Scoot!" she ordered. I dashed past her, giving myself the widest birth possible, and disappeared into the lounge to grab my schedule.

"Walter, I need this cleaned up by the time the children come in at 8:20. We don't need the students even more upset. We still need them to finish their reading fluency tests," she reported and then *clack-clacked* her way out the door and towards the gym.

CHAPTER FOURTEEN

After a long day, spending sixty percent of it outside on recess, playground, or dismissal duty, I couldn't wait to sit in the faculty lounge for five minutes in the air-conditioning and drink a large glass of cold water. When the last student was picked up from campus, I turned to go inside, anticipating the blast of cold air that awaited me, when Willa walked out carrying her tote bag and wheeling her case of school papers.

"Hey, Charli," she greeted, squinting in the sun. Her orange and black wide-leg palazzo pants danced in the breeze that stirred the heat wafting off the parking lot pavement.

"Hi, Willa," I said, trying to hide my exhaustion.

She smiled at my optimism. "Two more days; you can do it," she urged. The large gold sparrow pendant on her necklace danced across her sleeveless black blouse as she stopped in front of me and readjusted her tote bag. "You've been a big help already. You have no idea."

Smiling, I shielded my eyes with my hand and responded, "Well, I'm glad I'm doing something."

"Listen," Willa started hesitantly, "I hate to be the bearer of bad news, but Newton wants to see you as soon as you're done with dismissal duty."

I suppressed a sigh. So much for my five, quiet, air-conditioned, cool-down minutes in the lounge. "Thanks, Willa," I said, trying not to sound disappointed.

I took my time walking past the *We Are Alton Oaks*

mural and let the air-conditioned air erase the perspiration from the back of my neck. The mural depicted various parts of the school from the mid-1970's. The sad part was that besides the bell-bottoms and hairdos, not much had changed about the school. The playground still had the same swing set, the large metal slide that burned the back of your legs on a hot day, the jungle bars—where the cool kids sat at the top—and the bench that wrapped around the massive oak tree where the kids who'd rather read or talk spent their recess. The front office still had a young face popping out from behind the desk, and the gym still had a shelf full of basketballs, dodge balls, jump ropes, cones, and scooter boards that were wheeled underneath the bleachers for school events. The same basketball nets and scoreboard hung on the walls and the school library still had the same metal shelves, hovered around the eight tables in the middle of the room. The children in the mural were happy, though. Usually I'd say the same about the students at River Oaks Elementary School today, but there were a lot of somber faces around lately.

Before I turned the corner, I could hear Principal Newton's firm, straight-forward tone as she talked to a parent over the receptionist's partition. A second grade child sat teary-eyed and silent in one of the chairs in the small lobby, his head hung low as his feet dangled off the floor.

"Ms. Parker, please wait for me in my office. I will be there shortly," Principal Newton instructed, momentarily turning from a parent whose face was red from either embarrassment or anger, I couldn't tell which.

Nodding, I obeyed her instructions and relished the fact that I had a few moments to myself before having to stomach Principal Newton's criticism.

The air conditioner that sat in the window hummed, turning the air in the office ice cold. I closed the door behind me, hoping that the choice to conserve the chilled air to these four walls was the right decision and wouldn't lead to further head shaking on the principal's part.

As the whirlwind of the day died down and the growing frigidness of the air crept across my skin, I suddenly felt very tired and did not relish the long, hot walk back to the Alton house. Sinking into the uncomfortable wooden chair, I hoped that I wouldn't have to endure the principal's company for too long.

As the large, black-and-white clock ticked on, I watched the long, skinny, red second-hand make several trips past the twelve. Outside the window, through the slanted blinds, I could just see the leaves on the trees and that the sun's rays had made the shadows I saw on the baseball field at lunch grow much longer now.

Boredom soon took hold of me and I took to being nosy just to stay awake. I read once again over Miss Newton's diplomas from the University of Missouri and DePaul University. My eyes glanced over the spines of books and binders on the shelves. Her desk was tidy and neat. She had a cup holder with five sharpened pencils and another that held two blue pens, two black pens, two red pens, a yellow highlighter, and a black permanent marker. A desk calendar—perfectly color-coded—sat in the middle with two drop boxes above it. I assumed they were for incoming and outgoing files and paperwork. It suddenly struck me that there were no personal effects. Picture frames were absent along with any kind of personal stationery or décor. Many teachers had uplifting posters or signs— usually gifts from students—but none sat in Principal Newton's office. My eyebrows came together, finding the discovery quite odd.

With still no sign of Principal Newton, I leaned over her desk and began to take a closer look, wondering if there was anything that could tell me more about her.

Nothing. Absolutely nothing.

About to give up at Principal Newton's unbelievable perfectionism in the way her office was set up, I slumped back in the chair again.

Tick, tick, tick. The clock serenaded me from the spot next to the door when the moving rays of sunlight shed light on something. There was a small, 5 x 7 yellow notepad beside her desk calendar with nothing written on it, but if I leaned down and turned my head, I could just make out the indents of what was written on the previous sheet of paper.

I could have easily beat down this bubble of curiosity, but I was so bored that I let it take over. Many of the words were illiterate or written over so many times that it was hard to make out which letters went to which word. At the top, however, in a small space, as if it was written on a small post-it note, were the words "Money issues RE: De" and the rest of the message fell into the sea of unreadable garble.

Leaning farther over the table, I tried to read more, but bumped into one of the trays of paper. Shooting a glance at the door, I quickly tried to put the tray and its contents back in their perfectly placed space. It would be just my luck that Principal Newton would walk in at that moment, but she didn't. Moving the tray a fraction of an inch in either direction, I fussed with it until I thought it was perfect. That's when I noticed the letter at the top of the pile, written in small tight letters on loose leaf paper that was crumpled and bent in places from stuffing it into an envelope.

The letter was hard to read upside down, but certain words were printed in capital letters to get a point across: "I know you did it," "You will hear from my lawyer," and "You'll be sorry." My eyes floated down to the bottom of the letter and I turned my head to make out that it was signed by Lyle Woodridge, Dee Dempsey's fiancé.

The door swung open, making me jump slightly in my seat. "I apologize for keeping you," Principal Newton said as she walked in and closed the door behind her. A few wisps of blonde hair from behind her ears came loose from her French twist and seeing Ms. Always-Put-Together a bit worn made me empathize with her.

She took her seat behind the desk and scooted her legs beneath it. The red cardigan draped over the top of her chair peeked out from behind her and brought out her icy blue eyes. "It's no problem," I said, lying. Goosebumps rose on the back of my arms due to what I hoped was just the chilly air.

Principal Newton's eyes swept over her desk. "I wanted to talk to you about—" but before she could continue, the monotone two-beep ring of the telephone cut her off. "One moment," she remarked, reaching her manicured hands to the desktop phone.

"River Oaks Elementary, Principal Newton speaking," she answered. As she listened, she fiddled with the tray I had accidentally moved. Then she moved the pens in the cup beside the tray so that the like colors sat beside each other. Her eyes narrowed and her lips grew smaller as the person on the other side continued to talk. Though I couldn't hear what the person on the line was saying, I noticed that their tone grew in pitch.

"Mr. Woodridge," she interjected, cutting him off. "We've had this discussion several times. My condolences go out to you and your family, and if there is anything the school can do to help, please let us know. While I understand you are grieving, if you continue to call the school in these bouts of anger, I see no other choice than getting the police involved."

A few more words were exchanged on the other end of the phone call and then Principal Newton added, "If you decide that that's the best course of action, then please do. We will have our lawyers look at it too."

Without acknowledging a goodbye or waiting to see if he had anything more to say, Principal Newton hung up the phone. For no more than three seconds her eyes lingered on the receiver and I wondered if she was mentally going off on him as I had done several times to parents after I hung up on them after a honey-covered call home about behavior issues.

"Is Lyle doing okay?" I asked, testing the waters.

Principal Newton's eyes snapped from the phone to me, as if she'd forgotten I was there. "Mr. Woodridge thinks it's my fault that Ms. Dempsey is dead," she snapped. Her tone surprised me and I slid back in my seat. "But I think he's just shifting the blame."

"You think he knows who killed her?" I asked. It was my nosy Alton blood speaking; I heard the words coming out of my mouth but couldn't stop them.

"I think he did it!" Principal Newton snapped back. She pulled down on her blazer and adjusted the buttons. "They had been fighting after school, earlier in the week. They were fighting about the wedding. I had to ask the P.E. teacher to escort Lyle off the property and had to write Ms. Dempsey up for her conduct." Principal Newton pulled a file folder from her top right drawer and placed it on top of her desk calendar. "Look," she said annoyed. I had never seen or expected her to lose her cool and her behavior surprised me. Secretly, though, I didn't want her to stop divulging gossip. "It's no big secret that Ms. Dempsey wasn't my favorite teacher. I was hired here for results and she refused to give them. I hire people to teach and if the kids aren't learning, then the teacher isn't doing their job."

I thought back to her room full of manipulatives and teaching resources, and thought back to the inspiring conversation I'd had with her student Lindy and found that claim hard to believe. "She wasn't teaching? She just sat there in class everyday and did nothing?" I asked, noting how the tone of my voice sounded so offended by her claim.

Principal Newton selected a red pen from her cup holder, uncapped it, and began writing on a sheet of paper in the file. "She would teach the curriculum, but added all these bells and whistles and her class did not show as much growth as expected on the tests. These tests tell us if a teacher is doing their job."

"So if a teacher cares about each student and modifies the way they learn, and makes a safe and fun learning environment for the child, how does that show on the test?" I felt myself grow irritated; my heart thudded in my chest and my face got warm despite the icy air-conditioning.

"Through growth!" Principal Newton said, getting frustrated. "If the child is learning in a different way, feels safe and happy, then the child should show growth on these tests."

"What if a child is learning how to divide using objects instead of numbers in order to get the basic idea of division? How does that measure on a lengthy word problem involving expanded form and base ten diagrams? You can't expect a child to memorize random procedures and assume that they know the deeper content. From what I can tell in my three days on this campus, Ms. Dempsey was teaching the children the deeper concepts that would help them understand the *why*, not just the *how* of the concepts in the curriculum."

Principal Newton sighed and one of her eyebrows twitched as she continued to write on the paper in front of her. "If that were the case, we'd still be a D-rated school. It's all about numbers and growth. Please sign here," Principal Newton instructed, pointing to a dotted line and handing me a black pen.

"This is not a factory, it's a school," I said, signing my name with a bit too much force. "You can't expect teachers to just dump knowledge into a child's head and then expect the child to understand it like a computer program," I explained, realizing my free arm was gripping the wooden arm rest on the chair I was occupying. I let go when I realized my knuckles were turning white. "And what did I just sign?"

Principal Newton tore off the top copy, leaving the yellow and pink copies in front of her. "I'm sorry, Ms. Parker, but I've had to write you up for your conduct during this meeting," she explained, her voice adopting a calmer tone. "This copy is for you," she explained, handing it to me, "and these copies will be kept in your file and sent to the district."

Something in me snapped at that moment. Usually I would put up with the bureaucracy and politics because I needed to pay rent and eat, but I just couldn't put up with it anymore. I didn't *need* this job; maybe it was the universe telling me to follow a different path.

I stood up suddenly, the wooden chair scraping across the floor. Principal Newton looked up at me and having to look down at her was strangely satisfying. "In all my years of teaching I have never once been written up. I have spent countless hours fighting for my students and have lost many more hours preparing lessons, individualizing lessons, meeting with them one-on-one, planning field trips and activities and games. I've met with parents, have kept in touch with children, sat through countless hours of professional development that did nothing but waste the time I could have spent making my lessons better. You will lose more teachers running the school as a factory. You are teaching students to hate school and hate learning. You're supposed to be an advocate for children, not the tests. A real teacher will instill curiosity in a child, not stomp it out of them. I won't be a factory worker for you. I quit."

Without looking back, I left her office. I marched past the *We Are Alton Oaks* mural and swung open the door to the parking lot, letting the sunlight attack me. I walked out in a huff, squeezing my eyes shut periodically from the strong sunlight as I stomped past the two cars left in the parking lot and made my way back to the Alton House. *The nerve of that woman!*

CHAPTER FIFTEEN

As the sun was starting to tuck itself below the horizon in the heavy Monday night air, I was still steaming from the conversation I had with Principal Newton. Not one bit of me regretted what I had said, but the unjust attention those kids were getting really frosted my cookies.

I was so full of pent-up anger that sitting in the stifling house or on the porch with Mom and Bailey would not do well with my lack of patience, even more so considering that the argument I had had with Principal Newton was the newest town gossip. I threw on a pair of shorts and a bleach-spotted tank top and flew into the woods to burn off some energy and be alone.

As I entered the cool leafy canopy of the oak trees, my shoulders already felt lighter, though my head was swimming in doubt. When I had moments of stress, my head thought it was a welcome mat for doubts and unfair questions about leaving Jackson and moving back to Illinois. As my legs plowed through the path that had overgrown since Sadie and I had graduated from high school, a wave of pain, empathy, and tortured guilt came over me. As much as I tried to fight it, I felt hot tears begin to pool.

My eyes kept traveling to the blue sky, somewhere beyond the fluttering green leaves, in order to prevent the tears from spilling. While my mind was busy swatting away the demons of doubt that plagued my mind, the haziness that covered my reality cleared when

I found myself beneath a large, sprawling Bur Oak tree. That tree was as familiar to me as the corner store where other children spent their allowances on candy and magazines, or that ratty old teddy bear they squeezed the fluff out of as a child and found it years later in a box in the attic.

The tree looked old. Its gnarled branches were like crooked arthritic knuckles that reached out indecisively, twisting and turning in many directions. One thick branch hovered a few feet off the ground as it slithered through the air. As children, Jake and I would use skills acrobats would be jealous of just to sit and dangle our feet off it. Now, it seemed so insignificant; I could easily hoist myself up onto that branch. And as I began to feel the warm silent tears race down my cheeks, I decided to do just that.

As the dam broke and unbridled tears fell, I hoisted myself up. Alone, I let the tears fall, as long as they were silent. As long as I didn't moan in despair or curse the heavens above due to the pain inside.

The earthy scent of the forest, the sound of birds calling, and the cool air the trees provided kept me rooted in place, instead of towards the downward spiraling route my thoughts desperately wanted me to take. I knew I had to be an adult and take charge of my life: talk to Jackson, make a decision, get a job, move out of my parent's house... but I couldn't. I wasn't ready. I wasn't ready to face that unsure future—to go through more emotions and painful truths. Just a little bit longer under the wing of my parent's home and behind the curtain of Alton Oaks. I just needed a little more time.

The cracking of a few branches sharply turned my line of thoughts. With the back of my hands, I desperately tried to wipe any evidence of raw emotion from my face, but I could feel the puffiness around my eyes. As the rhythmic footfalls got closer, I could tell it was someone jogging the trail nearby. I sat still, hoping they would be too immersed in their music or pace to notice me. Closing my eyes, I hoped to blend into the forest.

As the footsteps slowed and the cracking of branches got louder, I knew whoever it was had stepped off the trail and spotted me. You can call it small-town hospitality, but I tended to lean towards small-town nosiness. Anger and dread shot through me. I did not want to share this space or moment with anyone. I just wanted to be invisible. This was *my* tree; my safe spot.

"Charli?" His voice was unmistakable. He looked at me confused, which turned into concern as he pulled earbuds from his ears and ducked under the thick sprawling branch to reach the front of the tree. His white shirt was drenched in sweat and his face was pink with exercise. It was a odd to see him without his uniform on; it seemed like he was always on duty.

"Hi, Jake," I said, faking a bright smile, but my voice tripped over the lump in my throat.

The dark blue shorts he wore just covered his kneecaps and I noticed how pale his legs were compared to the skin that wasn't usually covered by his uniform. "Are you okay, Charli?" he asked, tentatively. I was such an unpredictable time bomb of emotions that I didn't blame him for being hesitant.

"Oh, yeah," I said, waving my hand. "I'm fine. How 'bout you? How was your day?" I made sure that my voice was light and airy and ignored the dry scratches of my salt-stained eyes.

Jake came up beside me and leaned an elbow on the fat branch I sat upon. "Can't complain." He said the words as if he was brushing them out of the way to get to the real issue. Beads of sweat collected on his temples and one ran down his cheek as he added,

"You're the talk of the town right now."

The thumping music from his earbuds was faint in the space between us. "Oh?" I asked, my mind desperately trying to find a way out of this conversation.

"But, then again, when are you not?" he asked almost jokingly.

I jumped down from my perch, offended. "And what's that supposed to mean?"

Jake took a step back but his arm kept a hold of the branch I had just vacated. The nearby leaves still ruffled with the movement. He looked exhausted; his features didn't jump to the defense, instead his eyes dropped to the ground with a sigh. Remorse filled me for my over reaction.

"Geez, Charli," he said, deflated. "Nothing. I meant nothing by it." He turned his head back to the trail and added, "Not everyone is out to hurt you."

My heart fell. Of all the people in Alton Oaks, Jake was the one who would've checked on me out of hospitality instead of nosiness. As his feet shuffled through a patch of silent ferns, I called out, "Jake, wait! I'm sorry."

He turned and stepped back from the ferns without a word.

"I just... There's a lot going on. I can't. It's hard—" My sentence went in several different directions as I tried to apologize and explain myself. My fingers traced the rough grooves in the bark of the tree.

Jake walked back to the tree, twigs cracking below his feet, and asked, "Do you remember when we were younger and you and I would always try to climb this tree?" His hands grabbed onto the fat branch and he hoisted himself up. He glanced upwards which made the Adam's apple in his throat more pronounced.

"Yeah," I responded, watching him. I was grateful

for the change of topic.

Jake stood up on the fat branch, towering over me. His black and white shoes were inches from my hands and his weight made the branch move slightly. "Before Sadie moved to Alton Oaks, before Kindergarten, before we began growing up. And this branch was as high as we ever got." He reached for the branch above his head then pulled himself up with a simple chin-up until his legs dangled over it. "Do you want to see how high we can make it now?" he asked, looking down at me, lifting an eyebrow playfully.

I hadn't seen this side of Jake in twenty years and it brought a smile to my face. Kicking off my flip-flops, I pulled myself onto the fat branch and followed Jake up the tree in my bare feet until the branches were too thin to hold us.

We were at least twenty-five feet off the ground. Jake stood on a sturdy branch close to the trunk while his arms wrapped around a much thinner branch. Just below him I sat straddling a limb, a few feet from the trunk. My tender shoulder cried out in pain from over exertion, but I didn't mind the throbbing; it kept my mind on something else.

There was a small break in the canopy ahead where we could see the roof of the Alton House and one of the windows of my parents' bedroom. The world was different up in the canopy of our Bur Oak. On the ground was where my problems were. Up here my soul was quiet. Robins chirped from the surrounding trees and the breeze rattled the leaves in a song. The sweat that had collected under my tank top with the climb was picked up by the stumbling breeze and the sun was deep in the western sky.

"You know, Charli," Jake started as he moved to a limb closer by me. "You've got to be the only woman I know who would climb a tree barefoot."

My feet hurt from the rough bark, broken twigs, and friction of the climb, but I preferred that physical pain—especially as a distraction—to the emotional pain that almost made it impossible to breathe. There were a few scrapes and bruises yet to show, but it was worth it. "I might regret it tomorrow," I admitted, examining my dangling legs, "but I don't have anywhere to be tomorrow, so it doesn't matter." My face grew hard at the thought of Principal Newton's leadership style.

Jake planted himself on the branch beside me with his back against the trunk. Though I wasn't facing him, I felt his movements in the branches and saw the twigs up ahead dance with his movements. A long, lean branch coated in thick green leaves danced beside me with his shifting weight. Several moments passed before he spoke. "Do you remember our first day of Kindergarten?" he asked.

I looked back to see him with one leg dangling below him and the other propped on the branch, his knee bent. His gaze was lost in the gnarled forest of branches in front of him. He peeled the bark off a dead twig and let the pieces fall to the ground below.

"No," I said, turning my head and continuing to gaze north. Sadie had started school in Alton Oaks just after Christmas when we were in Kindergarten. I really had no school memories before her arrival.

"Oh, you couldn't wait to start school," Jake shared. "You were so excited. That morning you ran to my house—we planned to walk together: you, me, and our moms. I don't know why, but I was just so scared to start school. I cried all morning." I heard humor in Jake's tone and had to smile. "I sat on the couch and just bawled," he continued. "My mom tried everything to get me to shut up. Then your mom tried. Nothing. I remember clutching onto my Power Rangers doll like the world was ending. Then you crawled up on the couch beside me and took my hand and said, 'Don't be sad, Jake. I'll call upon the power of the saber-tooth tiger to protect you.' Then you pulled out your yellow Power Ranger doll from your backpack and put it beside mine. It was like you turned off a switch. I climbed off the couch and we walked out the door. We were halfway down Oak before our moms came running after us."

The tone of his voice was soothing, like listening to a bedtime story. I swung my feet and turned my body to face Jake. "How on earth did you remember that?" I asked, scooting closer to where he sat stoically balanced on a limb.

Jake broke the stripped twig he held in half and let both pieces fall. I watched as they hit and bounced from branch to branch until they landed in the dirt below. "Look, Charli, it's no secret that you've got a lot on your plate right now."

I saw where the conversation was headed and realized my only out was jumping. So, it was a serious injury—possibly death—or having this conversation with Jake. The choice was much more difficult than one might think. *Clever move, Jake.*

"Jake, please—" I started with a hint of panic in my voice. I swung my left foot over the branch, intent on beginning my decent to the ground.

"Charli, just hear me out," Jake said with authority. His feet moved to a lower branch, intent to follow me to the ground.

The fleeting look I gave him said *Please don't,* and *I don't want to do this,* but I kept silent as I lowered myself onto a branch and paused. I took a moment to secure the wall that kept back my emotions. The last thing I wanted to do was put it all on Jake. It was bad enough that Sadie got a handful of my confused and emotional teary-eyed nights while I hid away in her living room, far from the Alton House.

Jake planted his feet next to mine as we stood holding the same branch. I avoided his gaze, watching an ant crawl between my hands, and fought down the lump in my throat. "If you don't talk about it, you're going to explode," he said. "You don't have to talk about it with me, but I'm here if you need it. Just please, talk through it with someone and make some decisions before you snap."

The ant crawled over my hand and I fought the urge to flick it away due to its tickling feet. As the ant crawled off my skin and onto the branch, Jake began another sentence, but I cut him off. "I'll race you to the bottom," I challenged and began descending, despite my shoulder crying out in pain..

Jake's sigh wasn't at all discreet as he gave in and followed me down the tree, not racing at all. I wish I had had the strength to talk to him, to communicate with him, but I didn't. I lived on distractions instead of facing my issues.

As we climbed from branch to branch, I found myself thankful that Jake came across me on his run. He wanted that friendship we had as kids and I could use it, but I was too afraid to feel, too exhausted from eluding my feelings.

When my feet touched the dead leaves and broken twigs resting on the top soil, I watched Jake follow suit. "Beat you," I said, trying to sound cheery, as if Jake didn't just give me an invitation to pour out my heart.

"You win this time," he said, feigning defeat.

Maybe it was a peace offering or a door I wanted to leave open, but I gave Jake a short hug. Though his shirt was still damp with sweat and he smelled of deodorant, I knew if I held on to him any longer, I would start to cry.

Quickly, I pulled away and began to brush the debris

from my feet and slipped on my flip-flops as if the gesture had never happened. "Race you home?" he asked, his features not as burdened as before. I knew I didn't stand a chance in my flip-flops, but agreed anyway.

As I chased Jake's pace across the overgrown trail, in the dying light, I didn't realize how much I missed him until I came back to Alton Oaks.

CHAPTER SIXTEEN

Tuesday morning began in a puddle of sweat. It was already too hot and humid as the night grew into day and my shoulder was so sore, I knew I had to take some of the pills the hospital released me with. I knew both the pain and the temperature would only get worse as the hours marched on. Nevertheless, I tried desperately to sleep in, restlessly lying in bed with a fan blowing air on me until seven o'clock. Grudgingly, I peeled myself from the damp sheets and grumbled the whole way to the kitchen.

"You lived in Albuquerque," my mom said that morning as I complained between large gulps of water. "You should be used to this."

I only rolled my eyes when she wasn't looking. The dry heat of New Mexico was different than the humidity here. It was just too darn early in the season to be this hot in Illinois.

My mother was packing a salad in a Tupperware container before she left for work at the library. I don't know how she managed to handle food and bike to work and still keep her white capris pristine. "What are your plans today?" she asked, grabbing a jar of homemade salad dressing from a mason jar in the fridge and putting it in her black and green lunch bag. "Hanging out with Jake again?"

When Jake and I had emerged from the oak trees last night, Mom tried to get the scoop on what happened with Principal Newton, but I only told her I quit my job. With Bailey and Mrs. Kratsky watching from their perches on the porch, Mom kept trying to get answers until I feigned a headache and escaped to my room. I think she was really starting to take offense at the fact that I wasn't sharing enough of my life—the latest Alton Oaks gossip—with her. I'm sure this question was the beginning of a ploy for the answers she wanted.

Shrugging, I suppressed a sigh and pulled out a kitchen chair to take a seat. "I don't know," I shared. I was bracing myself for a storm of questions. A small breeze came through the kitchen window and I welcomed it as a reminder that freedom from her questioning gazes was near: Mom had to leave for work soon.

"If you're so uncomfortably hot," my mom said with a hint of irritation as she zipped her lunch bag, "go down to the river."

The thought of putting my feet in the river and feeling the near constant breeze that traveled with the current automatically appealed to me and began cooling me down. "Maybe," I said, already planning my day around the canal.

To my utter surprise, Mom only threw the strap to her lunch bag over her shoulder and waved in goodbye. I assumed her irritation about my tight-lipped life was really taking a toll on her. Sighing, I realized I was going to have to talk to her about something soon.

"Mom!" I called after her, suddenly struck with guilt. I caught up to her at the front door. She was in need of a hair trimming; stray locks fell into her eyes which made her jerk her head to the side.

"Yeah, Charli?" she asked with a sigh. Picking up her bicycle helmet from the hook on the closet door, she shifted her weight to one leg, moving her eyes down the floorboards in my direction.

My fingers played with the hem of the oversized t-shirt I had slept in as I searched for a sentence. "Mom,

I..." I started but couldn't finish. I wanted to apologize for not being as open as Bailey; to tell her my reservations were due to my personality, not because I was trying to be mean or evasive; to thank her for taking me in quite abruptly in April without asking too many questions despite her full-blown Alton nosiness; to let her know I'd noticed and appreciated her not pushing me for information about my adult life. There was so much I wanted to tell her, but nothing would form words.

Mom glanced at her watch. My heart fell with the notion that she had no idea of the emotions chaotically parading inside of me. "I'll see you in a few hours, Charli," she said flatly.

Through the screen door I watched her secure her helmet, place the lunch bag in the wire mesh basket, and kick up dirt as she left the driveway and pedaled down Oak Street.

Why couldn't I just communicate my feelings? Was that why my marriage had failed? Did Jackson become distant because I couldn't verbalize my love? My intentions? My own heart?

No. I shook my head. I wasn't ready for these soul-retching questions. Grinding my teeth, I climbed the staircase in search of a distraction.

As I eagerly walked out the door of the Alton House with my camera, a book, and a few snacks, I decided to check with Mr. K. and see if my bike was ready, instead of cutting through the oaks and Gnarled Circle Drive to the canal trail.

A few weeks ago, I'd dropped my old road bike off with Mr. K., the town's alternative bicycle fixer extraordinaire. He was much cheaper (and often friendlier) than the bike shop downtown directed towards the Canaries. Delayed by waiting for a certain part he'd had no luck finding in junk yards, he kept polishing and oiling the parts of the bike itching to come home with me. Traveling by bike was much more appealing in this weather than walking and I hoped Mr. K. had had luck on his last trip to the junkyard.

With my camera bag draped over my shoulder, and a tote bag of supplies in hand, I made my way down the driveway that spilled onto Oak Street. Desperately avoiding the sun and seeking the shade, I walked along the north side of the street, past Bailey and Jake's houses, and along the cemetery. There was no sidewalk on this side of the street, but I preferred gravel in my sandals to being sunburned with heat stroke.

When I reached the Kratsky house, I peered down the driveway to see if Mr. K. was in his workshop. Though the garage was open, his plump, overall-clad silhouette wasn't in sight.

Glancing at my watch, I noticed that it was just after nine o'clock. Mr. K. had probably just gone inside for breakfast after being available to kids on their way to school who needed a tire inflated or a chain greased.

I peered down the man-made trail to the canal, just behind the junior high where a cool breeze raced towards me. It beckoned me, drew me towards the cooler air near the water. I sighed and decided to visit Mr. K. another time and continued making my way to the canal.

Just as I made the turn around the school parking lot, where the trees grew thicker, I found a tall, thin boy in baggy black pants and a white t-shirt etching the first two letters of a well-known profanity into the trunk of a tree.

"Excuse me," I said a little forcibly as I came up behind him on the path. It's bad enough Alton Oaks now had a murder rate, but now this kid was messing with the wholesome minds of our youth. My hometown was better than this.

When the young man turned around, I quickly recognized him as Justin Willkens, the junior high kid with a knack for trouble whom Willa had scolded on my second day at the elementary school. He stumbled on a tree root and then leaned his back against the tree trunk like he had meant to do that. "What do you want?" he asked snidely, not at all trying to hide his pocket knife.

"Shouldn't you be in school?" I asked, gesturing towards the building about an acre away with a nod.

He rolled his eyes slowly—exaggeratedly—in response. Still grasping the knife, he let the point of the blade turn on the finger of his opposite hand, not yet drawing blood. He probably thought he was being intimidating, but it wasn't working on me.

Adjusting the strap of the camera bag over my shoulder, my patience about his attitude grew thin.

"Yeah, so? What are you gonna do about it?" he asked, taking a few steps toward me. I towered over him and I fought the urge to roll my eyes at his defiant attitude.

Coolly, I pulled the cell phone from the back pocket of my shorts. "I have the deputy's personal number in here as well as Willa Corden's. Who do you prefer I call first?"

He studied me as I scrolled through my contact list, probably trying to figure out if I'd really do it or if I was just trying to scare him. To really pack a punch, I added, "I'm sure the deputy would love to hear about this destruction of public property, or would it be vandalism? I'm sure the court would decide—"

"Damn, lady," he exclaimed. "You're worse than Ms. Dempsey." He closed the pocket knife and dropped it into his pocket, calling me an unsavory name under his breath. "I'm going," he said, walking towards the school, then stopped and turned. "Or do you need to babysit me to make sure I get there?" His voice dripped with impudence.

I waved my phone and replied sweetly, "Oh, no need. I'll just let the school know to expect you."

Once again he called me a five-letter word and disappeared around the corner of the trail.

Taking a few minutes to shift my state of mind, I closed my eyes and counted slowly to five. Sweat began to gather beneath my shirt, where my camera bag sat. As I continued my trek towards the breeze that played tag over the river, I sent Willa a text about finding Justin on the trail and to let the junior high principal know about it since I did not have their contact information. Before dropping the phone back into my pocket, I put it on silent. I needed a few hours without people to clear my head and focus on me. More specifically, I wanted to get lost in the distraction of photography, the river, and a few hours without worrying about personal questions people might ask me. I needed time to be invisible.

After spending all morning and a slice of the early afternoon hours sitting on a shady rock hidden from the canal path, my stress level plummeted. Reading through half a paperback, guzzling a crisp bottle of water, and gnawing on a bag of extra salty pretzels left me thoroughly distracted. As the river ran by and the wake from passing boats stumbled to the shore, I was relaxed and renewed. I found myself wondering how I ever survived living so long away from a body of water. Since I was a kid, trips to the river were always good for my soul.

The sun was strong, but starting to pass into the western sky. I guessed it had to be close to four o'clock when I started packing up my space. As I crumpled up my bag of pretzel crumbs and stuffed it into the bottom of the tote bag, I decided to walk home through Town Circle, crawling through the streets of the historic downtown. The cloudless, bright blue sky would make for a great background and give a lot of natural lighting and contrast to photographs of the historic part of town.

Stepping onto the canal trail, there were very few people around. One serious bicyclist raced past in his helmet and skin tight outfit while, in the distance, a woman with a stroller was heading east, towards Sheridan. I could see the clock on the steeple of Town Hall past the meadow and above the gardens that surrounded the Town Circle.

The building was laid out like a triangle, as were all the buildings in the circle, each a piece of a pie that made Alton Oaks work. The front of town hall was large—the biggest slice of the pie—and made up of three floors, nine windows on each, and two white columns that sat perched at the top of the stairs that led to the dark red front doors. As I walked up the canal trail, I could see the slim side of the triangle that looked out over the much smaller Parks & Recreation building. The large window on the top floor was where my uncle worked: the mayor's office.

Taking out my camera, I began snapping pictures of the way the steeple popped out from the climbing flower gardens, how it seemed to check on the roses that climbed up the lattice, and captured the way the river reflected in the window of the mayor's office. Adjusting the lens and switching to a manual focus, I was just able to capture my uncle standing behind his desk. The sleeves of his shirt were rolled to his elbows and he had the phone to his ear as he looked out over the river.

Circling the gardens, I saw Town Hall the way tourists first see it as they walk up Main Street. An older woman sat on the white stone steps of the building watching a small girl in a pink shirt and overalls hop up and down the stairs in measured movements. Taking a few more pictures that portrayed small town life, I began to wonder more about my great-great-grandfather who had been found murdered on these very steps ninety-six years ago. I began to wonder where exactly he had been found, who had found him, and why his murderer was never brought to justice.

A strong breeze ran past the gardens, sending a chill through the back of the foliage, sending the leaves and flowers into a gentle shudder. The blue, yellow, pink, and purple petals all seemed to wave their hands in my direction, snapping me out of my trance.

Walking west, I took a few more pictures of the Court House, which was nearly as big at Town Hall and sat beside it. The sun wasn't setting yet, but it was lowering itself into the western sky, making the courthouse illuminated from behind. I couldn't help but get lost in the sound of the shutter on my camera repeatedly go off, like the rhythm of a heartbeat. I crept past the Public Works building and the Visitors' Center—which was built like a cabin that overlooked the river—but my mind kept wandering back to Town Hall and what it had witnessed in all of Alton Oaks' history.

Circling back to the front of Town Circle, I made my way down Main Street, turning back a few times to capture the old-fashioned light posts and citizens resting on benches in the foreground of the historic buildings. As the streets started filling with citizens who usually ventured to the gardens or the canal path with their families after work, I decided to take a less populated way home. I carried myself quickly up Maple Lane, holding my breath as I passed the large reflective windows on the library in hopes that my mother wouldn't see me so I didn't have to deal with an awkward exchange.

Maple Lane lead me to the elementary school where I crossed the vacant playground, slipped between houses and across Gnarled Circle Drive, where I dived into the oak trees of my childhood, hoping to steal a few more moments of solitude before reaching the Alton House.

"Charli!" My head snapped up from my feet along the forest floor as I automatically recognized Sadie's voice echoing through the trees. Her voice sounded slightly frantic and my stomach dropped.

"Sadie?" I called, surprised to hear her wandering through these trees, calling my name.

"Charli!" she exclaimed, stomping through the underbrush, still dressed in her pink polka-dotted, sea green scrubs. "There you are!" Tripping over a raised root, she stumbled but caught herself on a branch. "Why haven't you been answering your phone? Are you okay?"

Sadie was out of breath and harried. I knew something was amiss other than me ignoring my phone. "What? I'm fine. What's wrong?" I asked as I pulled my phone out, seeing that my home screen was filled with notifications from Mom, Bailey, Sadie, Jake, Alex, Jillian, and, of course, Jackson. "Oh, wow," I said under my breath at the volume of missed calls and voicemails.

When Sadie reached me, her mind was suddenly distracted and she caught a glimpse of my bruised and scraped legs. "Holy hair ties, Charli!" she exclaimed. "What in the devil's dill pickles happened to your legs?"

Sadie must have been upset because she was using an extraordinary amount of her g-rated swears. Before I could explain that the injuries were from climbing a tree, she continued her original train of thought. "Never mind." She quickly swatted away the concern and grabbed my hand. "Everyone's looking for you."

"For me?" I asked as Sadie started pulling me north, towards the Alton House. Utter confusion soaked my features as I blindly followed her.

"Yes!" she said incredulously. She then slowed her pace and turned to me and asked, "What exactly happened?"

"What do you mean?" I asked confused. "Like what happened with Justin Willkens this morning?"

Sadie stopped and rooted her feet to the ground, concern and intrigue filling her eyes. "What exactly did happen, Charli?"

"What the heck do you mean?" Though we were standing beside each other, our communication was miles apart from making sense.

Sadie's blue eyes studied my face for a moment before she licked her lips and said slowly, "You don't know?"

"Don't know what? Did I get Justin into trouble? Did he do something else?"

"Something else? Justin? What in blue blazes does Justin have to do with this?" Sadie asked as if I was purposely keeping the conversation off-topic. Sadie's head tilted to the left and her eyebrows grew closer together as they often did when she was confused—the look I always saw on her face when I would meet her outside the advanced math classes her dad used to make her take in high school.

I had had enough with the lack of communication between us and said, "Sadie, what in the world are you all up in a huff about?"

Sadie sighed which straightened out her posture and her eyebrows. "It's Principal Newton," she shared, looking for a hint of recognition in my face. When my gaze gave her nothing but confusion, she crossed her arms over her chest, suddenly uncomfortable. Her eyes danced between a rotting log covered in patches of fungus and my feet.

When she finally did meet my eyes, she reported, "She never showed up to school today. Then someone noticed her car in the parking lot. She was inside, slumped over, strangled with the seatbelt. It was still around her neck." She paused as my mouth hung open in a gasp. "Charli," she said, taking a step towards me, "Principal Newton is dead."

CHAPTER SEVENTEEN

The air in my lungs whooshed out in surprise. Another murder? What was happening in Alton Oaks?

"You honestly haven't heard? Where have you been today?" Sadie asked, taking my hand once again pulling me towards the Alton House. My shoulder began to ache once more.

"Nowhere. I just wanted some me-time. Hold on," I said, pulling my arm from her grasp and raising it, as if to stop any more words coming from her mouth. The camera bag slid down my shoulder and I adjusted it. My brain was still trying to wrap my head around the news. "Why is everyone looking for me?"

Sadie took a deep breath and bit her bottom lip. Her eyes flitted between my feet and hers as she hesitated. "Well," she began, dragging out the word. "Because people are thinking that you were the last person who saw Principal Newton alive."

The world rocked on its side for a moment and I grabbed Sadie's shoulder. "Me?" I asked. I could only imagine the implications people were coming to in this tiny town. My stomach started flip-flopping with the thoughts.

Sadie continued to bite her bottom lip and nodded. "The janitor was the last to leave the school and he said you were in Principal Newton's office, waiting to speak with her and Principal Newton was in the middle school wing doing her surprise classroom inspections."

Despite the news of her demise, a fire lit beneath me with this information. Principal Newton knew I was waiting to speak with her—under her own request—and yet she let me wait for close to an hour!

"What would I know?" I asked, agitated. "When I left we—oh!" It struck me that when Principal Newton and I fought, I stomped away from the school clearly upset and fuming: a good motive for murder.

"Yeah," Sadie replied as if she had read my thoughts. "Jake really needs to talk to you," she stated. After a few beats, Sadie linked her arm in mine for support as we quietly made our way down the old footpath until we reached the profile of the Alton House.

Jake sat on the wooden bench beside my parents, who sat quite still on the porch swing. Dad was still in his work clothes and I realized that he'd pulled himself from his work for this. This was serious.

"Charli, where have you been?" my mother asked concerned. She sprang from the swing and pulled me into a hug as I reached the top of the stairs with Sadie. "We've been looking for you all over town."

Jake tipped his wide-brimmed deputy's hat in greeting as I sat in the rocking chair. I let the tote bag fall onto the floorboards with a thud and then gently placed my camera bag beside it. Sadie stood leaning against the wooden railing, quietly observing the scene with her hands crossed over her chest.

"I went down to the river, like you suggested," I told my mother. The wooden rocker creaked as I shifted uncomfortably. My glance shifted between my parents and Jake, who had his Steno pad resting on his knee.

"Charli, I rode my bike up and down the canal path for hours trying to find you," my mother shared, glancing at Jake uneasily. She then clutched the locket on her necklace, looking quite dramatic, and added, "I thought the worst—" She couldn't finish her sentence and guilt, once again today, soaked through me.

"Listen, Charli," Jake started, leaning forward, pulling out his Steno pad. I could already tell that this wasn't the Jake I climbed a tree with yesterday. This wasn't friend-Jake visiting, this was work-Jake, here on police business. My shoulders slumped at the realization. "The janitor at the elementary school discovered Principal Newton's body in her car around noon today." Jake caught my gaze and held it for the next sentence. "And it seems as though you were the last one to see her alive." Jake let the information sink in for a few moments before he added, "I need you to tell me exactly what you did today."

I looked down at my hands, biting my bottom lip in thought, as I began nervously picking at my fingernails. "Well, I woke up at around seven this morning and came downstairs for breakfast with Mom—"

"That's true!" my mother exclaimed. She nodded at Jake as if it could clear my name from the suspect list. Jake momentarily lifted his gaze from the pad of paper to my mom and then back to me.

I continued, "Then about an hour later I left the house. I was going to hang out by the river and take some pictures."

"And did you go to the river?" he asked.

"Yes."

"Which route?" Jake leaned forward and licked his lips. For a moment I caught a glimpse of friend-Jake, which calmed my nerves, however slightly. "I need you to be as descriptive as possible with where you went, who you saw, and what you did."

Taking a deep breath, I described walking down Oak and past the Kratsky's house, hoping to run into Mr. K.

"Did you get to speak with Mr. Kratsky?" Jake asked, his pen hovering over the paper.

"No. School just started so I figured he was having breakfast. Mrs. K.'s golf cart was in the driveway and the garage was open."

"What happened next?"

I picked at a hangnail on my thumb as I tried to conjure as many details as I could. "I walked down the footpath, behind their house, and came across Justin Willkens. He's a seventh grader at the junior high. He was carving the letters *F* and *U* into a tree on the path behind the parking lot." I explained our exchange of words, mentioning the knife and that he headed towards the school and that I texted Willa about it.

"Who is Willa?" Jake asked, momentarily looking up from the notepad.

"She's a sixth grade teacher at the elementary school. Willa Corden." I took a moment to bite the hangnail on my thumb, nervously.

"And why did you text her if Justin attends the junior high?" Jake asked without looking up from his scribbling.

I described the interaction between Willa and the boy on my first day at the school. "I also don't have the number for the junior high," I explained.

The corner of Jake's mouth dipped and I wasn't sure if that was good or bad. "What then?" he asked.

"Between the football field and town circle there's that small patch of oaks, you know?" I asked, hoping he was following my descriptions.

He gave me a curt nod and I continued. "Across from that, on the other side of the trail there's that big Weeping Willow tree. Just past it there's an outcropping of rocks and I sat there and read all morning." I tried hard to read Jake's face as I talked. I tried to capture a twitch of realization or a movement denoting a break or clue that changed everything, or a wince that gave me a hint of whether or not I was a serious suspect. Jake, however, gave nothing away. His stoic note taking was frustrating.

I snuck a glance at Sadie who shifted uncomfortably from her perch. The wooden railing creaked with her inability to sit still. Her eyes were fixed on the table between us. She ran the pendant on her necklace back and forth as the thin chain played on her lips.

"Did you see anyone? Talk to anyone? Did anyone see you?" Jake asked with the smallest hint of desperation in his voice.

It then hit me: my yearn for solitude on the morning Principal Newton was murdered—especially after our argument the night before—did not look good for me. Not only did I have a motive, but now I had opportunity. "No," I admitted, deflated. "Not until I went to Town Circle to take photographs."

"What time was that?" Jake asked.

"Just after four, I think."

"What were the photos of?" Jake asked, scooting forward from his place on the bench.

"Just hometown stuff: the Town Circle, town hall, the gardens, the courthouse, the river, people..." I trailed off trying to remember if I saw anyone I recognized.

"Can I see your camera?" Jake asked, tucking the Steno pad back into his pocket.

I reached down and opened the padded camera bag and pulled out the most prized possession I owned. Hesitantly, I outstretched my arms until Jake grabbed the camera. He looked at the buttons carefully and turned it over with care. Finally, he looked up at me so I saw his eyes instead of the top of his deputy's hat. "Can I take the memory card, Charli?" he asked like a friend who could help, and didn't demand it with authority. That small gesture released some of the tension that had built in my shoulders.

Nodding, I reached out and took the camera. Opening the side door, I ejected the SD card and handed it to Jake, cradling the camera in my lap.

"Charli," Jake said as he stood. "Can I have a word with you?" He nodded towards the other side of the porch. I stood at his request. "Yeah." I handed my camera to Sadie who let her necklace fall to its place below the collar of her shirt. I followed Jake to the stairs on the other side of the front porch. The creaking of the floorboards seemed too loud at our pace.

"Listen, Charli," he started and I turned to face him. His broad shoulders and deputy's hat drowned out my view of Sadie and my parents. Concern filled his chocolate brown eyes. "You had an argument with Principal Newton yesterday. Best anyone can tell, you were the last person to see her alive." He put a warm hand on my shoulder for emphasis and added, "This is serious. I need you to be careful. As a friend, I strongly recommend you not be alone until this gets figured out."

I leaned back on the pillar at the top of the stairs, worried about how this day had panned out. "Do you really thing I could've committed this murder, Jake?"

He swallowed and emotion flashed across his face for the briefest second before it went back to business. "It's not important what I think. What's important are facts."

My shoulders slumped with his answer. Did Jake really think I was capable? He said yesterday that I needed to work through issues before I snapped. Did he think I had snapped? "You'll clear my name, right Jake?" I asked, hoping for a glimmer of hope that he had my back.

Jake took a breath that was filled with words he didn't want to say. Hesitation weighed heavily on his eyelashes as his eyes swept the floor and an uneasy hand rubbed the back of his neck. "I will collect the facts, Charli," he finally said.

I had been biting my lips, feeling his indecision. "And when you do," I said, still feeling the sting of his words, "You'll see I'm innocent."

"Charli, I—" he started, tucking away his deputy mask, but was cut off.

Sadie stepped into our bubble then and put an arm around my shoulder. "If you knew Charli at all, you'd know she would never do anything this heinous. It's ridiculous that you can't even recognize that."

"Will I be under arrest?" I asked, highly concerned.

"No," Jake said quickly. Sadie's words had gotten to him and he tried to adjust his features. "There's no evidence, just suspicion. Please be careful, Charli," he said, slipping on a pair of aviators that reflected the hard eyes of Sadie and me in front of him. "And don't leave town. I'll be in touch."

As Jake walked down the stairs and to the police bicycle that often cruised the canal, my mother rose from the porch swing, pulling my father with her. "We are going straight to Jillian to see about a lawyer," my mother announced. Her black padded bike shorts were wrinkled with the humidity and Dad still wore his black trousers and long-sleeve dress shirt—though the sleeves were rolled up to his elbow and dark patches of sweat were beginning to form around his neck and under his arms. I could only imagine how uncomfortable he was, but didn't hesitate to follow my mother. As they hopped onto their bicycles and pedaled down Oak, Dad led the way.

Sadie kept her arm around me and, despite the added heat it added to my side, I was thankful for it. My life was beginning to feel like a house of cards near an open window. Sadie was the hand that blocked the breeze that luckily kept it constructed... for now.

The sun dipped lower into the west and Sadie let out a long sigh. I couldn't have agreed more. Despite Jake's advice, I didn't want to be careful; I wanted to clear my name and I didn't care how dangerous that road could be.

CHAPTER EIGHTEEN

The sound of Jillian's metallic gold electric scooter she rode around town was only noticeable when its tires crunched on the driveway and the headlights lit up the blue door of the small shed she parked it in overnight.

Sadie and I were lounging amongst the shelves of potted herbs and fairy lights on Jillian's screened in back porch as my cousin bounced up the stairs. "Seeking refuge?" she asked, tucking her helmet under her arm. Locks of her brown curly hair spilled over her shoulder with the movement.

I nodded. Sadie had suggested we spend the night at Jillian's house in order to avoid the unusual number of people visiting my mother's front porch for details on the hottest town gossip: me. "Do you mind?" I asked from the spot I occupied on the multi-colored cloth hammock.

Jillian shook her head with a smile. It was the same smile she would give me when I'd come home from school and tell my big cousin about passing a math test or getting a part in the school play. "Not at all," she said, leaning against the bannister. "Want some tea?" she asked, looking between Sadie and me with a hint of exhaustion painting the lines on her face. "I need some," Jillian muttered more to herself than us and disappeared through the back door, letting drafts of cold air roll over our faces.

"I think we should head out first thing," Sadie suggested, continuing the conversation we were having before Jillian came home from work.

"Sadie," I said with a sigh. "Go to work. I don't need a babysitter."

Sadie had been looking up in the rafters from her perch on the canvas chair swing. Her eyes were following a firefly that snuck in with us and danced with the fairy lights. Now she sat up and leaned forward, making sure she caught my eye. "I *know* that, Charli. But everyone thinks my best friend is a murderer. I'm with you one hundred percent—to prove your innocence," she clarified, "not to commit murder."

I rolled my eyes in good humor. "Sadie," I said in protest again knowing full well I wasn't going to win this argument.

"I have like ten vacation days, Charli," she cut me off. Her eyebrows arched and her bottom lip pouted. It was the puppy dog face Brett Murphy couldn't say no to in high school when he was behind the counter at Froz T's and Sadie asked for free sprinkles or an extra scoop on her ice cream taco. "Please," she started. "Let me help. I'll be the Watson to your Sherlock, the Hastings to your Poirot, we'll be the heterogeneous Nick and Nora Charles of Alton Oaks until we clear your name."

Dramatically, I let out a sigh that sent tendrils of my hair flying above my forehead. "Hey," I interjected with sudden realization, "where were those ten vacation days when I was in Albuquerque?" I asked, changing the subject.

"Well..." Sadie trailed off and leaned back in the chair. She pulled her feet up so that her chin rested on her knees. The swing she sat in began to turn away from me without her feet as an anchor.

"I hope chamomile is okay," Jillian said as she stepped onto the porch, saving Sadie from an awkward conversation. "It's been one of those days," she added, placing the tray on the sunflower-shaped folding table.

"What happened?" Sadie asked, jumping at the chance to change the subject once again.

"Oh," Jillian started as she sat heavily on the canvas swing, adjacent to Sadie. "There's been issues with Living Wills with a few clients."

"Dee Dempsey's will?" Sadie asked. She placed her feet on the ground and leaned forward, very interested in Jillian's answer.

"Maybe," Jillian simply said, her Yellowstone National Park mug, centimeters from her lips. Her eyebrows arched scandalously as she took a sip. I knew she wouldn't reveal anymore information and disappointment coated Sadie's features. She leaned back and let the swing twirl her attention in another direction.

Sitting up from my place on the hammock, I reached for the mug with a grizzly bear emblazoned on the side. "Did my mom and dad come by today?" I asked.

"Yeah..." Jillian trailed off. She tucked one leg beneath her and let the other anchor the chair. Her bare toes dragged slightly on the dusty floor.

"And?" I arched my eyebrows in question. Even Sadie turned her chair around to face Jillian as we waited for an answer.

Jillian let her mug rest on her thigh and her eyes swept across the floorboards. "Well, Mr. Westbrook is always here if you need his legal services, Charli, but I wouldn't worry about it too much right now. Mr. Westbrook is aware of the suspicion against you, but that's all it is, kiddo. There's no concrete evidence pointing the blame on you. I honestly wouldn't worry."

I didn't realize I had been holding my breath until it all rushed out in relief. Her words made me feel slightly better. "I wish Jake was as confident as you are," I admitted. My fingers tickled the rim of my mug as doubts began to cloud around me once again.

"Jake thinks you're guilty?!" Jillian nearly spat out her tea in disbelief. "The deputy? Isn't he your friend or secret lover? No wonder you're so borderline paranoid."

"No—What?—Not necessarily," I tripped over my words, not sure which of her sentences to tackle first.

"Oh, he does so!" Sadie chimed. "He practically said so."

"What?" I shot Sadie an incredulous glance. "No he didn't!" I argued.

Sadie's lip twitched—she was holding back words which was incredibly difficult for her. I turned my attention back to Jillian. "He said the same as you: there's no evidence against me, just suspicion."

Jillian relaxed and melted back into the chair, nodding slowly. Her eyes dashed between Sadie and me as she lifted the mug to her lips again. Jake always seemed to be a hot button for Sadie.

"And he is not now and never has been my 'secret lover.' I wish people would stop spreading that rumor," I mumbled from behind the rim of my mug.

Maybe normal girls could catch their husband cheating on them and rebound or get even with an old friend, but not me. My heart still hurt. My chest grew tight, a lump expanded in my throat and my eyes prickled with the threat of tears. When would this raw pain end? Was I destined to live with it every empty moment of my life?

"Have you..." Sadie's voice broke through my tortured world. Her big blue eyes finished asking the question she didn't speak aloud. A few times over the past couple weeks she'd suggested that I contact Jackson—the healing would start after decisions were made.

I shook my head and a lock of my overgrown bangs escaped from a bobby pin. "One bullet at a time,

Sadie," I said and tucked the stray piece of hair back into place. "My priority right now is to clear my name."

Though Jillian's house had air-conditioning, I fell asleep on the hammock on the back porch. Sadie slept in the canvas chair swing, hugging a Tibetan bowl she found fascinating. As she fidgeted with it throughout the night, the bowl would vibrate echoing tones, letting me know I wasn't alone.

After raiding Jillian's stash of caffeinated teas, we set out to retrace my footsteps of that day to see if it jogged any memories that would lead to clues. We were naïvely optimistic.

After changing into a pair of Jillian's clothes, I found Sadie packing her pajamas into her duffle bag, dressed in a black tank top, matching leggings and a black baseball cap that held her hair back. "What are you wearing?" Sadie asked as I descended the last stair.

I had thrown on an old t-shirt that Jillian usually gardened in and a pair of jean shorts I needed to wear a belt with. "What?" I asked, looking down at my garb.

"You have to go incognito," she said, gesturing at her wardrobe.

"Sadie," I said exasperatedly and I passed her to pick up my mug of cold tea. "I'm not wearing black; it's a million degrees out."

As I downed the rest of my tea, Sadie sighed. "Fine. At least wear the hat," she instructed, plopping it on my head, weaving my ponytail through the hole in the back.

I rolled my eyes as I grabbed my wallet from the dining room table and followed Sadie to the front door.

"So what's the plan? Where to first?" Sadie asked as our feet pounded the sidewalk outside Jillian's house.

The sun beat down on our backs momentarily until we reached the shade of the row of massive weeping willows that ended at the Kratsky's house. Sadie grabbed the crook of my elbow to slow my pace as we reached the Kratsky's front lawn. "You definitely don't want to go into town. Everyone's talking about you."

I didn't respond. On a mission, I heeded her words silently and turned down the footpath where the air still held the cool temperature of the night. I wanted to check out the parking lot. I had learned from my mother that with one school day left and no principal, and a suicide, the school board had voted to dismiss the students early and not have them come in for their last day—a half day. This meant the parking lot and the school's grounds would be empty unless a teacher wandered in for last minute belongings.

"I want to check out the parking lot," I finally shared, determined, as we stood on the border of the parking lot, still under the shade of the trees. To the far right I could see a lone car, Principal Newton's gold sedan, sitting in the middle of yellow DO NOT CROSS police tape that swayed lazily in the breeze, like a hammock on the beach.

"I dunno, Charli," Sadie said as she scanned the vicinity. "We need to be careful. And it looks pretty official." Sadie darted out in front of me before she finished her sentence, to be sure I was listening to her. "And the tape on the perimeter clearly says *DO NOT CROSS*."

I could sense Sadie's foreboding and tried to relax my facial features to reassure her. "Relax. We're not going to cross, just investigate."

Sadie bit her lip and looked around once more. She was clearly more concerned than I was about potential gossip that would arise if anyone were to see me at the crime scene, sneaking around. I was glad one of us was.

"Come on, Watson," I said, grabbing her elbow as we emerged from the trees and into the sunlight of the blacktop. "I swear not to cross the tape," I promised.

"Or touch anything!" Sadie added adamantly, increasing her pace to keep up with me. "And only for a few minutes. You don't want anyone to catch you out here, Charli."

Sadie tugged on my arm so that I stopped and caught her eye. It wasn't fear or desperation that filled her gaze, but concern. Concern for my reputation, my innocence, my well-being. "When you say, 'Let's go,' we're gone. Promise," I said.

Sadie nodded with a deep breath and we continued walking down the parking lot towards the car surrounded by yellow police borders. If a car could look as guilty as a one-night stand, this one did. The gold four-door car sat quietly beside the red brick building. There was no sign posted that the spot was reserved for the principal—in fact, none of the spots were reserved, not even for handicapped. Geez, had it always been that way? Has no one ever needed ramp accessibility before?

I walked the perimeter of the yellow tape to try and get a better view of the interior but there was nothing to see. No books or briefcase. No coffee mug or crumpled receipts. There wasn't even a garbage bag. "Sadie," I said, motioning her to me. She was looking towards downtown, hoping no one would come around the corner. When she got beside me, she followed my gaze into the car. "There's nothing inside. Nothing."

"What did you expect? A signed confession from the killer?" she asked sarcastically.

"No, but she was the principal. You'd think there'd be books or papers, or a briefcase, a backpack or something!"

"The police probably took it," Sadie said, her eyes still scanning for a stray gossiping citizen.

"Still," I said, crouching and scanning the ground for

anything out of the ordinary. Sweat began to gather on my forehead, just beneath the band of the cap. I took it off for a short reprieve as I stood up. "Something's just..." I trailed off, trying to find the right word and weaved my ponytail back into the cap.

Not right. Off. Wrong. Amiss. No word could accurately describe the wrenching awkward feeling in my gut. I guess I should be thankful that my name wasn't written in blood across the dashboard.

Sadie must have sensed my uneasiness because as I studied the front seat, she stopped looking for nosy neighbors and came to my side. "Okay, let's take a step back," she suggested. "We know she died here and the police combed the scene for clues. Let's look outside the box." She grabbed the crook of my elbow and turned our backs on the vehicle. "Which direction would she have come from?"

Lifting my hand, I pointed south, to the corner of the elementary school. "From there, I guess. It's how all the teachers get in and out."

"Okay," Sadie said with growing animation and pulled me along the building which was fully exposed to the intensity of the rising sun.

Stopping before the dumpsters, she turned to me and hypothesized, "The attacker could've potentially hid here. She never would've seen him."

"Him?" I asked, raising an eyebrow. I wondered what gossip she had collected from the Alton Oaks Citizen Watch Facebook group that my mother had formed after Sara's murder in the spring. I refused to accept the invitation as it was just another way for the town to gossip.

Sadie rolled her eyes as if she didn't have time for such a question. "Well, we know it's not you and statistically it's more likely to be a man." She returned her gaze to the massive green containers whose scent grew stronger with the heat of the day. She jumped, desperately trying to peer over the bins and said, "Now see if you can find anything, any clues."

Standing beside Sadie, I lifted my scope of view by standing on my tippy toes. "It's empty," I reported, trying to keep my balance while not having to touch the dumpster. "There's just a broken ruler, a Buzz Coffee shop cup, and a few stained papers."

"Stained in blood?" Sadie asked hopefully and peered around the dumpster.

"No," I said, rolling my eyes. "And I'm not jumping in to investigate it only to find it's expired mayonnaise from the cafeteria that's baking up something fierce in the sun," I added before Sadie could suggest that I hop inside. Her face fell slightly but then resumed looking for clues, squatting between the dumpster and the building.

After a few minutes I sighed and stood, stretching my back muscles. "I don't think there's anything here," I reported.

Sadie stood too and tried not to look dismayed. Her eyes scanned the trees in the distance behind me that hid the footpath to the canal. "Okay, then who could be a potential witness? Who has visual access to this point in the parking lot?"

With hands on our hips, we scanned the perimeter, not able to see a roof or window from the Kratsky's or any of the houses in the distance on Gnarled Circle Drive. From the south, trees separated the parking lot from the playground and playing fields. The trees were thick with leaves. This parking lot had almost perfect cover.

Sadie and I walked north, back to the car. There was a patch of trees; the Kratsky house, and the junior high before we reached Oak Street. The only place not tucked away under the cover of trees was the driveway entrance to the parking lot on Sheridan Avenue. Peering down the drive I was able to see Allyson's house—a girl from high school who lived next door to Sara's murderer. For a moment I wondered if Jim really was the murderer and not his wife, but quickly brushed the thought away with the memory of his wife stabbing me in the back with metal sewing shears. Subconsciously, I cradled my arm as my shoulder still carried pain from the injury.

"Hey, look," Sadie said, tucked into the corner, out of view from Sheridan Avenue. I crouched down next to her. A few shards of broken glass glinted on the blacktop. Our heads simultaneously traveled up to the broken security light above us. Despite the heat, a chill crept down my spine and I wondered if the police had noticed this detail. Without the security light, the parking lot would've been hidden under the cover of darkness. Even if some witness had been on the footpath that night, they wouldn't have been able to see a thing.

We stood to get a better view of the broken light and jumped when the burly face of Walter, the school's custodian, appeared in the small, grungy window to our left that I could only guess came from his closet/office. Immediately, he pulled a cord so that the blinds would shut with a fluttering thud before us.

"Now," Sadie said, grabbing my arm and walking. "It's time to go. Right now," she urged, pulling me along with a hint of fear in her voice. "Something is definitely not right."

CHAPTER NINETEEN

When Sadie and I returned to the Alton House (using old footpaths to avoid being seen), we nearly shrugged off all the heebie jeebies our morning venture had delivered. The sun was in full force, high and mighty above our heads when we climbed the noisy, rickety stairs.

As usual, Mom, Mrs. Kratsky, and Bailey were on the porch in their usual spots: Mom and Bailey on the swing and Mrs. Kratsky pushing herself back and forth on the wooden rocker. A bulbous, sweating, glass pitcher of lemonade sat on the table and Sadie and I didn't hesitate to pour ourselves each a glass.

As Sadie disappeared into the house to retrieve two glasses from the kitchen cupboards, I purposely sat on the bench beneath the living room window and asked, "So what's up in Alton Oaks? What's the scuttlebutt?"

One-by-one, confusion coated their faces as they exchanged glances. Yes, normally I wasn't one for gossip, but I was on a mission to clear my name. Any little tidbit could help.

"Scuttlebutt?" Bailey asked, the ice in her glass clinked as she placed it back onto the table.

"Yeah." I nodded. "The latest news. What's going on around town?"

"Besides two more murders?" Bailey asked incredulously.

Brushing away her attitude, I turned to Mom and asked, "What's going on at the library? Anything new on your Facebook page?"

Mom studied me wearily and I half expected her to require a quid pro quo for information since I've somehow always managed to keep key details and gossip from her. As a show of faith (and to prove I wasn't jesting their need for gossip), I quickly offered, "The security light in the school parking lot is broken. The bulb was smashed."

Surprise widened her eyes.

Sadie had come out of the house and shot me a confused look as she handed me an empty glass. I hoped years of friendship would enable us to read each other's minds so that she'd understand the angle I was playing at, but I don't think it worked. I wasn't going to share our run-in with Walter, and I didn't want her to either. We needed to keep some chips in our back pocket. Besides, Walter was going through enough—he didn't need more gossip and more speculation without evidence. No matter how many chills our recent encounter gave me.

"Well," Bailey began with amusement lighting up her features. "The latest 'scuttlebutt,'"—she used finger quotes to further demonstrate how ridiculous my choice of words were—"Is that you've been carrying on a relationship with an underage boy, Justin I think his name is, and you murdered Principal Newton out of unrequited love so that no one could keep you two love birds apart." As Bailey talked, her voice got higher with false dramatic interpretation.

My mouth hung open in utter disbelief. I couldn't decide if I should laugh or rant about how ludicrous that claim was.

"This town is ridiculous," Sadie replied, but fished out her cell phone, undoubtedly checking the latest gossip in the Alton Oaks Citizen Watch Facebook group.

With a smirk she couldn't hide, Bailey shrugged.

"Apparently Allyson saw you disappear on the footpath behind the Kratsky's yesterday and minutes later Justin emerged, and then they found Principal Newton dead in the car."

"Honestly," I said, rolling my eyes and refilling my glass of lemonade. Before I could go on about how ridiculous this whole story was, my cell phone started going off.

I didn't want to look, in case it was Jackson, but when Bailey asked coolly, "Aren't you going to answer that?" I didn't want to explain my hesitation.

When I saw it was Jake calling, I sighed away a bit of tension that had collected in my shoulders. Despite the doubt Jake had in me, I was relieved to see it was him calling and not Jackson. Springing up from my seat, I walked towards the stairs as I answered. "Hey Jake," I greeted, sitting down on the top stair so that only my legs were in direct sunlight.

"Hey Charli, I have good news, and some not-so-good news," he reported. Bustling sounds of a busy police station played in the background.

"What is it?" I asked. I noticed how quiet it was on my side of the line and saw all four women leaning towards me, their eyes fixed on my lips as if they could read them. I turned away and watched the canopy of the oak trees flutter in an unfelt breeze as Jake spoke.

"The good news is that the coroner put Principal Newton's death between five and seven o'clock Monday evening, not Tuesday morning." Relief flushed through me and I felt that familiar lump in my throat, only this time it was from relief. Finally, I was catching a break!

"And the not-so-good news?" I asked.

"I need you to come into the station and tell me exactly what you did yesterday from the time you left the school until I saw you in the oaks."

I quickly realized that there was a short chunk of time where I had no alibi. "Surely I still can't be a suspect."

"Charli," Jake said with a sigh. "It's like someone lit a match and boom, the town is crawling with gossip and things people thought they saw, and people drawing incorrect conclusions."

"What about Dee's murder? Is it just forgotten now, or is it still being ruled as 'a suicide?'" I was starting to get upset. I felt like the entire town was getting off-track from what really mattered and I couldn't stop it.

"No. No," Jake said, trying to stop me from getting upset. "But it's a classroom. There are a ton of fingerprints and hairs in the room. Nothing definitive yet. We can't catch a break."

I listened and tapped my feet against the wooden planks of the front porch anxiously. Due to Jake's tone, I pictured him sitting at his desk, hunched over, piercing the bridge of his nose between his thumb and forefinger. "Listen, Charli," he started again, "it's best we take care of this thoroughly and completely, by the book."

I sighed and held my head with my free hand. "All right," I agreed. "I'll be right over."

Slightly defeated, I lumbered back to my glass of lemonade where I was met by four quizzical looks, dying for more information. There was no way I could back out of this one. I had to give up some gossip in order to get out of there.

Quickly I downed my lemonade and placed the cup on the tray with the sweating pitcher. "Principal Newton died Monday evening, not Tuesday morning," I reported.

"So, then, you're off the hook!" Mom said enthusiastically, picking up her glass like she was cheering a toast.

I squinted, trying not to give away too much. "Not quite. Jake asked me to meet him at the station to clear all this up," I explained, inching my way towards the stairs.

"Clear what up?" my mother asked, realizing I was escaping without giving away too much information.

"I promise I'll come right back, I'll explain more then. I need to talk to Jake first," I said with a hint of desperation in my voice as I took off down the stairs and sprinted down the driveway.

"Wait for me!" Sadie called. She downed her lemonade and chased after me. "Don't leave your Watson behind!"

Sadie and I managed to avoid seeing any citizens—besides a few kids riding their bikes down Sheridan Avenue, probably heading to the school playground or basketball court. When we rounded the corner of Oak and Main, we were hit with crowded streets of citizens on their lunch breaks. Surprised looks, raised eyebrows, and whispers haunted our every move. Sadie, the one who usually stopped to chat when she could, only grabbed my elbow and ushered me further down the street until we reached the doors of the police station.

Despite the central air-conditioning that the building installed in the mid-nineties, it was still stuffy inside. Box fans sat in corners of the wooden floor and circulating fans sat on desks and the tops of filing cabinets, giving the illusion of cooling breezes that chased away the damp perspiration below the brim of the baseball cap I still wore.

As usual, Seth Granger was behind the front desk but only waved us in as he talked to another man whose face was studying a manila file folder. For the most part, we were ignored by officers on the phone or typing away on the computer. No one thought that murders would be a normalcy in Alton Oaks, but here we were: in a police station not yet used to the manpower it takes to secure, study, and solve these horrendous crimes.

Jake was standing at his desk, the phone resting on his shoulder as he recorded notes on a yellow legal pad with a pencil. I noticed the teeth marks below the eraser as he scribbled. "All right, thanks, Al. I'll be in touch," Jake said and hung up the phone.

"Charli, thanks for coming," Jake greeted as he ripped the paper from the pad and folded it in fourths.

Before I could respond, another officer approached Jake from behind and handed him an inter-department envelope. "We got another call about the boy," he shared as if it was the hundredth call of the kind that day. "Someone heard him threaten her outside school that day."

Jake sighed, his eyes sweeping over Sadie and me before responding. "Thanks, Bill. Call Willa Corden and ask her to come in. She's been taking over at the school. Oh, and make sure this gets to the Chief," he instructed, handing the officer the folded paper. "Follow me, please," he instructed, motioning us to follow him to the far corner of the station.

He opened the door to a small room with a table and a few chairs. It wasn't anything like the interrogation rooms on the television. The walls were painted light blue and there was a framed picture of the station, circa 1940, hanging on the far wall. There was, however, a small security camera installed in the northeast corner of the room.

Sadie and I sat on the same side of the table. There was a box of tissues and a blue, plastic Alton Oaks Annual Polar Ice Plunge cup, sporting a plate engraved with the year 2012, which held two pens and a broken pencil. "Thanks again for coming down," Jake said, scooting his chair closer to the table. "We need to formally question you about what you were doing between the hours of five and seven on Monday evening." Taking out his Steno pad and the pencil he had tucked behind his ear, he said, "I would like to ask you a few questions before we begin."

I nodded. "Okay."

"Do you know Justin Willkens?"

"Isn't he the junior high kid?" I asked, knitting my eyebrows together.

Jake nodded.

"I've only met him once or twice,"

"How long have you known him?"

"I met him on Friday when I was outside the elementary school with Willa. She was confiscating a lighter from him. Didn't even introduce myself. Then yesterday, when I was walking to the river, I came across him on the footpath."

"And what happened then?"

I shrugged. Very matter-of-factly I stated, "He was vandalizing one of the trees and I told him to go back to school or I would call the police and the school."

"Was it a heated confrontation?"

"No. He was a regular kid with a lot of attitude. Called me some names under his breath and I pretended not to hear. He eventually stomped off back to the school and I texted Willa about it."

"Willa Corden?" Jake asked, looking up. His eyebrow arched with the question.

I nodded. "She's the sixth grade language arts and history teacher at River Oaks."

Jake scribbled something onto his notepad before he asked, "What about Principal Newton? Did she ever threaten you?"

Shaking my head I responded, "No."

Licking his lips, Jake took a few moments before he

asked, "Did you ever threaten her?"

"No." I said quickly, defensively. I thought back to our heated conversation and wondered if I had accidentally threatened her, but I didn't think so. I wasn't that type of person... was I?

"What exactly happened before you left the school on Monday?"

"Principal Newton and I had a disagreement and I quit my job." When I realized that I was flourishing my hands too much, I sat on them.

Jake tapped the chewed eraser of the pencil on his notepad, letting a few seconds feel like a few hours. There was no fan in this room and with the door closed, it was getting stuffy. Sadie sat quietly beside me and focused on the conversation intently. "What did you argue about?" Jake asked.

"Well, Lyle Woodridge called and Principal Newton was upset. She went on about how Ms. Dempsey wasn't a good teacher and that good teachers are measured by standardized tests. She wrote me up for my behavior—when, really, I was just disagreeing with her and standing up for Ms. Dempsey. Then I quit and left." As I finished the sentence, I was suddenly aware of how tense and upset I was. Having been written up for my actions just before Principal Newton's murder couldn't have helped my case. Sadie touched my shoulder momentarily which made me take a deep breath and relax.

Jake finished writing notes and took a deep breath. He did not put the Steno pad away and I knew this wasn't over. "As specific as possible—and this is important, Charli." He made eye contact with me and held my gaze as he continued, "Please tell me what you did Monday between the hours of five and seven P.M."

I had been chewing on my thumbnail as Jake talked and now set my hand back in my lap, nervously picking at my fingernails. Looking up at the framed photograph of the police station on the wall, I collected and organized my thoughts. "At around 3:30 I got off duty at school and Willa told me Principal Newton wanted to see me. She—Principal Newton—had me wait in her office for about an hour before she finally came in, around 4:30 or so. We had our disagreement and I left at around five o'clock."

"Did you see anyone? Anything out of the ordinary?" Jake said, his gaze imploring for more information—as if my innocence depended on it.

Biting my bottom lip, I tried to replay the memory like a movie, but I couldn't get past the frustration I felt that afternoon. Shaking my head, I answered, "No. I walked out of her office and down the hall. There was nobody there. Nothing out of the ordinary. I walked into the parking lot and went home."

Jake's lips pulled to one side of his mouth as if I had let him down. "What about on the way home, did you see anyone?" Sadie asked.

Both Jake and I turned our heads to her, as if we forgot she was there. "Which route did you take? Did you see any bikes or cars or strollers?"

"I went through the parking lot towards the footpath—" I explained.

"Did you see any cars in the parking lot or hear voices on the footpath? Did you see Principal Newton's car?" Sadie asked. She leaned over the arm of the chair as if to enter the bubble Jake and I had been in.

"I think so. I remember there were two cars in the parking lot. One was green or blue. Small-ish. The other one could have been Principal Newton's. I don't remember."

"What happened next?" Jake asked.

"I took the footpath to the east side of the Kratsky's house and walked up Oak Street. But I didn't see anyone or come across anyone. It was hot out."

"What time did you arrive home?"

I glanced at my watch. "It usually takes me about half an hour to get home in this heat. So probably around 5:30. When I was upstairs changing my clothes, I heard Mom and Bailey's voices downstairs. They were talking about the newest town gossip involving the janitor and me. Mom usually gets home from work around 5:30."

"Did you talk to them or see them?"

"No. Well, yes. I didn't talk to them. I was still pretty upset about what had happened with Principal Newton so I ran past them on the porch as I headed out into the oaks around six."

Jake leaned back in his seat and put his pencil down on the table. "And I came across you at six-thirty."

It felt like several minutes had past while Jake processed this information.

"Well that's not enough time for Charli to go to the school, kill Principal Newton, and come back," Sadie remarked.

Again Jake and I turned our heads in her direction and I stopped picking at my fingernails. "You said Principal Newton died between five and seven o'clock," Sadie explained. "It sounds like Charli has an alibi between 5:30 and 7 except for the half hour in the woods before she ran into you. That's not enough time," Sadie argued.

Jake lifted an eyebrow in response as he skimmed his notes. "It still leaves a large chuck of time from 4:30 to 5:30 where Charli doesn't have an alibi."

I groaned. "So I'm still a suspect?"

Jake gave a curt nod. "You're not the only one, if that's any consolation." He stood up. "Excuse me for a moment," he said and grabbed his Steno pad before he left the room.

As he closed the door behind him, the blinds on the window swung back and forth. "Why doesn't he trust you? How could he think you could still be a suspect?" Sadie asked with her arms folded over her chest.

"He's just doing his job," I shared truthfully, watching the blinds come to a halt. "I'd rather have Jake on my side than not."

Sadie was about to say something when the door swung open and Jake walked in, studying his notes. "You can't tell me anything more about the cars in the parking lot, can you?" he asked, leaning forward in his seat.

Again, I tried to play the memory back in my head but couldn't. I shook my head. "I'm sorry, Jake."

Jake forced a smile and nodded his head. "Call me if you do, okay?"

I nodded.

"I'll be in touch," he said, standing once again. "Thanks for coming in."

"That's it? We're done?" I asked, standing and pushing my chair in, hearing it scrape across the wooden planks.

"For now." Jake nodded and held the door open. Sadie exited first and, as I walked out, Jake's arm grazed across my elbow to grab my attention. "Be careful, Charli," he said.

"Jake?" I asked, hesitantly as I watched Sadie walk ahead of me.

"Yeah?" he said closing the door behind him.

"The janitor, Walter. Have you looked into him?"

"The janitor?" he asked, walking slowly beside me to his desk. "There are rumors. Why do you ask?"

Biting my lip, I tried to form a sentence in my head before I said it aloud. "Something's not right."

"With the janitor?" he asked as we approached his desk. He put his Steno pad down and I noticed the voicemail light on his phone was blinking rapidly.

"I'm not sure," I admitted.

Jake put his hands on his hips, just above the belt that held his gun. "I'll look into it, Charli. Promise," he said and put his hand on my shoulder reassuringly. "We're close. We'll figure this out."

CHAPTER TWENTY

It was close to two o'clock when Sadie and I walked into the shade of the Alton House. My right hand pulled on the old rope swing hanging from the tree in the front yard as we passed it. Mom, Bailey, and Mrs. Kratsky were still on the front porch, with Jenna now sitting on the bench.

The pitcher of lemonade was filled with ice and brimming with a new batch of juice. A box of Girl Scout cookies sat opened beside it. "You were right," Sadie said as we climbed the stairs and she made a beeline for the lemonade. "It's way too hot to be wearing this much black." Filling her empty glass, she chugged her first helping of juice.

"So?" Mom asked, eyeing me and leaning forward in her swing.

Oh yeah. I did tell her I'd fill her in when I got back, didn't I? I grabbed a cookie and sat beside Jenna on the bench, fully aware of how much I was sweating from walking across town. Twice.

"What did Jake have to talk to you about?" Bailey asked, straightening out her sundress.

I swallowed the last bit of the cookie and Mom filled my lemonade glass, handing it to me with interest. "He needed my alibi," I admitted.

"I thought you were off the hook because she died on Monday instead of Tuesday?" Mom asked.

"With all the rumors going on around town about me, I am still a suspect. And I don't have an alibi between 4:30 and 5:30 yesterday."

"Well that's not a very big window if Principal Newton died between five and seven o'clock," Sadie explained.

"Those approximate times of death are pretty accurate, as I understand," said Mrs. Kratsky. "It all has to do with maggots and flies, according to Dr. Mark Sloane."

"Who is that?" Sadie asked. I'm sure as a nurse at the hospital, she had a pretty good idea of the doctors there.

"From *Diagnosis Murder*. Been watching a lot more episodes since Sara's murder. That Dick Van Dyke can put his shoes under my bed any day," Mrs. Kratsky said and gave a mischievous giggle. Even I couldn't help but laugh at her retort.

"I've been wondering about that," Mom said, dismissing Mrs. Kratsky's chatter. We all looked at her inquisitively as she put down her glass of quickly-melting ice cubes. "If Principal Newton died that night, why didn't anyone discover her body that morning? I'm sure parents and kids and teachers walked right past it."

"It was parked at the entrance of the parking lot, by the Sheridan driveway," Sadie shared absentmindedly as her thumb scrolled over the screen on her phone. If I was closer, I would have kicked her to warn her from oversharing, but that fact distracted me. Why hadn't anyone spotted her in the car?

"Well, apparently, when they found her, she was slumped over the front seat. She wouldn't be seen so easily just passing by," Bailey shared as she waved to her husband's car pulling into their driveway. Her charm bracelet glinted in the sunlight as it slid down her wrist. I could just make out Eli's head in the backseat of the car, bouncing around as Carter pulled into the garage.

"Not to mention, everyone avoided her like the

plague," Mrs. Kratsky added.

I nodded in agreement, remembering how teachers would flee at the sound of her *clack-clacking* heels in the hallway. I wouldn't doubt that they avoided parking near her car too.

"Who did find her?" I asked.

"The janitor," Mom offered. My stomach sunk. "His name is William or Willis or Wallace. Something of the like."

Sadie and I exchanged glances, but shared nothing of our run-in with him that morning.

The crunching of gravel in the driveway diverted our attention from gossiping. A young teenage boy in a Prescott's Grocers uniform was peddling his bike up the Alton driveway with a front basket overflowing with flowers.

"Well, what do we have here?" Mrs. Kratsky asked in a sing-song voice as we watched the boy. Flowers being delivered to the Alton House? That was potential gossip!

"Good afternoon," the young boy offered with small town charm. He wore a Blackhawks cap and beads of sweat traveled down his cheeks from his temples.

"Hello, Evan." My mom smiled in greeting and offered the boy some lemonade. "How's your mother? Feeling better I hope?"

Evan took several long gulps of lemonade, leaving both the glass and the pitcher empty. He held the basket of flowers with one arm on his hip. A small breeze tickled the petals, sending their perfume tripping across our noses. "Oh, she's much better, Mrs. Parker. The soup Mrs. Kratsky brought over on Monday got her out of bed and back to work."

"Works every time," Mrs. Kratsky said with a hint of pride. "I'm so glad to hear that."

"I have a delivery here for Charli Parker," Evan

informed, extending the basket in my direction but did not shorten the distance between us by moving his feet. I half wondered if it was due to the rumors of Justin and me, or if Evan thought I was capable of murder.

"Me?" I asked, confused.

He nodded, still extending the basket in my direction.

As I stood to take the flowers, my stomach plummeted. *Please don't be from Jackson*, I thought to myself, pleading with any deity that was listening. I had been thoroughly distracted from my failed marriage for the past week and did not need a nudge in that direction right now, especially with such an audience.

"Who are they from?" Bailey asked, leaning forward from the porch swing as Evan hopped down the stairs to his bike.

Sadie stood beside me and grabbed the card tucked between the stems. I was glad she did because I was too afraid to.

I watched her face as she read the note. Instead of anger, frustration, or impatience reflected in her expression, it showed confusion.

She glanced at me with her eyebrows raised and her gaze clouded in tangled thoughts while the women on the porch watched us impatiently. Leaning over her shoulder, still hugging the basket, I read the handwritten note:

> Charli,
>
> Whether the rumors are true or false, thanks for being on Dee's side. That despicable woman got what was coming to her. No matter what the circumstances, you make this world a better place.
>
> Lyle Woodridge

"Well?" Bailey asked expectantly, tucking a lock of her long blonde hair behind her ear.

Sadie silently handed the note to my mother. My sister hungrily read it over her shoulder. "Such indecency," my mother commented and handed the card to Mrs. Kratsky.

"How cryptic," Mrs. Kratsky responded and handed it back to Sadie.

"It's like he sent you a thank you card for murdering Principal Newton—which you didn't!" Sadie said, looking over the note once more.

"I bet he did it," Bailey mused.

"Kill his own fiancé?" Mom inquired.

"They did fight just before it happened," Sadie added. "About postponing the wedding."

I nudged Sadie with my elbow as Mom nearly choked on her melted ice cubes.

Mrs. Kratsky, taken aback, sputtered, "What?" I started to wonder if Sadie kept anything I told her a secret.

Sadie sent me a look of regret that my mother caught onto—yet more town gossip that I didn't share with her.

"It was just something Principal Newton told me that night," I shared defensively. "She had to write Ms. Dempsey up and the P.E. teacher had to escort Lyle off campus. It happened after school one day," I added, regretfully.

"But why?" Bailey asked.

I shrugged. "I honestly don't know."

"Charli," my mom began seriously. "I would head straight to Jillian with this note and speak to a lawyer. It sounds like someone is trying to set you up."

Sadie took the flower basket from my arms and set it on the bench behind us. "Your mom's right. It's time to see a lawyer. I'll take you."

Sadie's father used to be a successful lawyer in

Alton Oaks, but had clients as far as Chicago and Springfield. Some of that legal knowledge must've rubbed off on Sadie... at least I hoped it did.

I nodded and followed Sadie past the unusually quiet group of women on the porch. As we departed, once again, down the Alton driveway, I had an odd feeling that I wouldn't see that house again for a while. I hoped that it was just nerves and not intuition deflating my self-confidence.

CHAPTER TWENTY-ONE

As Sadie and I reached the populated corner of Oak & Main, more and more faces turned to look at us, but no one offered a smile or greeting. I did not like this feeling at all.

Passing the people outside the bank and the church seemed to take forever. A sigh of relief escaped my lips when we saw the law office of Westbrook Attorneys nestled between the firehouse and the police station.

The building looked the same as it did years ago, when I tagged along as Sadie checked in with her father after school or when her mom had us deliver care packages of muffins or banana bread when Mr. Wilder and his staff had long days at the office.

The large dark-tinted street windows showed the waiting room occupants, the people walking outside and the art gallery and boutiques across the street. There was a receptionist's desk across from the waiting room chairs with a small hallway and four offices hidden in the back. However, now that Mr. Westbrook had taken the property over, the paint was a calming blue and the wooden accents were varnished a deep walnut, instead of a stark '90s white.

As we stepped inside, I was surprised and a bit comforted that the air still smelled the same: strong coffee and potpourri that tried to cover the smell of fresh paint.

"Hi, is Jillian Alton in?" I asked the young woman behind the receptionist's desk. She was balancing the phone between her ear and shoulder when she looked up at us. Her fiery red curls danced as she held up a finger, signaling us to wait a moment. Sadie and I exchanged silent, worried glances as we waited. Finally, the woman hung up the phone and asked, " Do you have an appointment?" She shuffled through papers on the desk before her heavily blue eye-shadowed eyes met ours.

"No. I'm her cousin, Charli. Is she free?" I asked, hopeful.

Recognition registered in the woman's eyes as I introduced myself. "She is sitting in on a conference call right now. It might be a while," she shared.

"We'll wait," Sadie said with authority. The woman nodded and returned to her work, but I couldn't help her surreptitious glances as we sat.

Sadie and I didn't notice the woman in the corner chair, sitting beside the ficus, when we first walked in. Her long brown hair was draped over her shoulders as if it was a reassuring hand of a friend, while fresh tears rimmed her red eyes. She didn't look up as I sat beside her and Sadie sat on the other side of the ficus. Her hands kept wringing a tissue that was already falling into pieces onto her black skirt. "Veronica?" I asked, leaning towards her, "Are you all right?"

Her head snapped up as if she was caught doing something she wasn't supposed to be. She looked as though she was painfully keeping so many things inside of her, a blocked dam of emotions. "Oh, sorry. Charli, right?" she asked.

I nodded. "This is my friend, Sadie. I'm not sure if you've met," I introduced.

Veronica gave Sadie a shy nod and returned her gaze to her tissue. "I'm sorry," Veronica apologized. "I'm just a mess. I'm finalizing some of Dee's legal matters before I head back home."

"I am sorry about your loss. You won't stay a little

longer? Until Dee gets justice for her murder?" Sadie questioned.

Veronica's head snapped up once more. "Murder?"

Sadie looked at me as if she spilled the beans, but the rumor—or truth—had spread all over town by now. "With the principal's death, a lot of people believe Dee's death was on purpose," Sadie explained.

Fresh tears rose to Veronica's eyes and I wanted to kick Sadie to urge her to stop gossiping with Veronica. The woman was clearly suffering. "I'm sorry," Sadie said, realizing what emotions she stirred, and grabbed a tissue from the box on the table with old magazines.

"Oh, no. It's not you," Veronica said and grabbed a new tissue. "It has been a hard week with the funeral, taking care of Dee's belongings, and Lyle. He is not handling this well. I don't want to leave him before he even starts grieving."

"Before?" Sadie asked, confused. She glanced at me and I shot her a look to stop with the intrusive questions.

"He hasn't cried. He's just so angry. I need him to move on. To find closure and grieve," Veronica explained as she wiped her eyes once more.

"Veronica Dempsey," the receptionist cut in. "Mr. Westbrook is ready to see you now."

Veronica nodded. Grabbing her purse, she turned to me and said, "Charli, I'm truly sorry about everything you're going through with this unfortunate series of..." She paused as fresh tears sprang to her eyes. Dabbing her eyes with a cheap tissue that crumbled into pieces over her eyelashes, she cleared her throat and added, "You're carrying a cross that isn't yours."

I put a reassuring hand on hers and replied, "If there's anything I can do for you or Lyle, please let me know. Don't feel like you have to rush out of Alton Oaks. We're here for you."

Veronica forced a smile and nodded before standing. We watched her shake hands with Mr. Westbrook, who wore a smart suit and vibrant tie, and disappear into a back room. Suddenly, I was even more nervous about what my future might hold with this case.

I turned to Sadie because she could always make me feel better. "Oh!" I said suddenly, realizing Veronica had left a manila file folder tucked into her chair. "She must've left this behind," I said, reaching for the folder and standing.

With a sense of urgency, I grabbed it and turned, ready to explain the situation to the receptionist. The last thing Veronica seemed to need right now was misplaced documents. Unfortunately, I made a spectacle of myself when many of the documents dropped out of the envelope and I bent over to pick them up. They quickly scattered across the wooden floor. Sadie helped gather the documents and tucked them back into the folder as the bemused receptionist watched, a penciled eyebrow raised. "Sorry," I explained to the receptionist as Sadie fiddled with getting the papers inside. "Veronica left these behind; can you get them back to her?"

I turned to Sadie whose nosiness couldn't be helped and was reading one of the pages before placing it in the envelope. I plucked it out of her hands and handed the envelope to the receptionist who quickly scurried to a room in the back.

"Honestly, Sadie," I whispered as we sat back down. This time Sadie took Veronica's seat so that we sat beside each other. "Can't you control yourself?"

Not seeming to hear me, or because she was feeling awful about being chastised, Sadie sat on her hands and looked at the floor. Minutes crawled by and the crackled sound of an easy-listening radio station played from the speaker behind the ficus. When the receptionist returned, she sat down in her chair with a grunt.

"Are you okay?" I asked, turning to Sadie, who looked solemn. "You look like you're the one under suspicion of murder."

Sadie came dangerously close to an eye roll and then maintained her composure. "Just thinking," she replied, swinging her feet in the chair and looking at the carpet near the entrance of the waiting room. "Processing," she clarified.

After several more minutes of listening to the muffled sounds of the street behind us, Sadie popped out of her chair and asked the receptionist a question I couldn't hear. "I'll be right back," Sadie said as she returned to where I sat. "I need to make a phone call."

I only looked at her questioningly, wondering what she was up to. I watched her go out onto the sidewalk and dial someone on her phone. When she caught my gaze, she gave me a reassuring smile and turned her back to me.

Sighing, I picked up a magazine and leafed through it. After finishing an article about the International Space Station, I was surprised Sadie hadn't returned. Turning around, I couldn't find her anywhere on the street. I suddenly felt very alone.

I tried not to panic about where she had gone, why she had left, and the overwhelming sense of solitude I was feeling. How did I live so long without her? Picking up another magazine, and another, and another, I read empty articles, breezed past full page advertisements, celebrity photographs, and barely caught the scent of perfume samples tucked between the pages.

"Excuse me," I said, rising from the chair. The skin on the back of my thighs stuck to the leather chair, despite the air-conditioning that gave me goose bumps.

The receptionist raised her head as if she had forgotten she wasn't alone. "Is Jillian available yet?" I asked, approaching the desk. I rested my arms on the cool surface as I looked down on her red curls.

"I'm sorry, hun," she said, picking up the phone. "Let me check on that for you." Some of her mascara flaked off and dusted the skin below her eyes.

"Thanks," I said, wondering if I should send her a text. And Sadie. Where was she?

A small ding echoed through the space signaling the opening door. I turned, relief beginning to wash away some tension, thinking it was Sadie. Instead, Jake and the police chief walked inside very formally. There was no friendly smile on Jake's face and the Chief's hands hovered over his wide belt, near the handcuffs. My stomach fell.

"Charli Parker," Chief Gomes started. "You need to come with us."

CHAPTER TWENTY-TWO

The receptionist's hands hovered over the phone, not yet dialing for my cousin. Her eyes danced from the chief, to the deputy, and to me. I wished she would get her. Whatever was about to happen next, I didn't want to be alone.

I trusted Jake. I really did. But he had a job to do and I knew him well enough to know that he didn't let his personal life affect his job. I should have asked questions. I should have talked to Jillian first. But I trusted Jake. "Okay," I simply said, knowing the weight of that word.

To my relief, the Chief did not pull out his handcuffs. He extended his beefy hand and led me next door, to the police station, while Jake followed. As soon as Jake opened the door to the police station, all eyes followed us. The world seemed to move in slow motion as we walked past the front desk and through the sea of desks with whirling fans. I was led into the interrogation room I was in earlier that day. Only this time it felt smaller.

I walked around the table and sat in the red vinyl padding of the metal chair. My soul seemed to deflate with the movement. "Wait here, Charli. We'll be with you shortly," Jake said before closing the door.

I sunk lower in the chair with the metal sound of the door knob clicking in place. The stark loneliness closed in on me like a claustrophobic in a padded cell.

Chewing on my thumbnail, I eyed the security camera in the corner and wondered who was watching.

Why were they watching? Why was I here? What was going on and what had happened to Sadie?

My leg began to shake up and down nervously, as questions without answers swarmed through my head. After biting my thumb raw, I moved onto another finger.

The wristband on my digital watch had broken about a month ago when I went fishing with my dad and it fell into the river. My dad bought me an analog watch and the ticking seconds filled the room like a medieval audience waiting for a hanging. Once in a while I'd hear a voice outside the door and I'd brace myself for a visitor, but none came. The second hand of my watch continued to be my only companion.

I had just about run out of fingernails to gnaw on when the door finally opened and Sadie was ushered inside. Jumping from my chair, I hugged her as if her absence had been months. There was a prickling behind my eyes and I pushed away the urge to cry. "Where have you been? What is going on?" I asked as Sadie pulled out a chair and sat down.

Sadie looked grief-stricken, sick. She kept running her top teeth over her bottom lip, nervously. "They said your lawyer should be here shortly," Sadie replied, unable to meet my gaze.

Sitting down beside her, I asked, "What's going on?"

Sadie's features struggled to find an answer to my question. "Oh my god," I said, letting my imagination get the best of me. "Am I going to jail?"

Looking up, I saw pain in Sadie's eyes as they met mine. She shrugged. "I don't know, Charli. I don't know what happened."

Her eyes raced back and forth between the plastic cup of broken pencils on the table and the tissue box. "I thought I found a clue. I thought it would save you. But now everyone is so tight-lipped and upset. I think I might have messed up," she explained.

"What clue? What happened?" I asked.

Sadie stopped biting her bottom lip and I could see how raw it had gotten. "In that folder," she explained. "You didn't see?"

She must have meant Veronica's manila folder. I shook my head; being a murder suspect distracted me from my regular Alton nosiness.

"One page—the one you took out of my hands—I didn't read it all, but it looked like a ransom note or a threatening letter or something. All I saw was the words '$50,000' and 'alibi.' Then I started thinking about the other pages I picked up. There was a picture—it looked like it was taken by a P. I. or something through the blinds of a room. It was Dee and Veronica together. I don't know what it means. It could be nothing. Something from their childhood or their parents, or college. I don't know." Sadie took a breath and her forehead wrinkled in worry. I put a supportive hand on her back.

"I called my dad," she continued, "to get his advice. But I decided to talk to Jake anyway. I don't know what it all means, but I hope I didn't put nails in your coffin. I would never be able to forgive myself."

"What do you mean?" I asked. "It sounds like you're saving me!"

Again, pain creased her features. "There's one more thing," she explained.

"What's that?" I asked, wondering how I could be at fault for any of this.

"That note I read?"

"From Veronica's file?" I asked, clarifying.

Sadie nodded. "It had your name in it, too," she said.

CHAPTER TWENTY-THREE

"How?" I asked. A typhoon of dizzying questions filled my head. How in the world did I get in the middle of all this? I barely knew Dee, Lyle, Veronica, and Principal Newton. Maybe my mother was right and somebody was setting me up.

"Charli, I'm sorry. I can't—" Sadie was cut off as the door opened. Jake had his hand on the knob as Mr. Westbrook walked in. He wore a deep blue tie that didn't make his gray suit look so depressing.

Jake's expression gave nothing away. In fact, he avoided gazing into the room as much as he could while he let Mr. Westbrook in and then closed the door, leaving the three of us alone. My stomach dripped with acid as I realized that Jake might not be on my side through all of this. He would always be on the side of the law. And, really, I couldn't be mad at him for that... but I was.

"Ms. Parker," Mr. Westbrook said, shaking my hand. He set his brown leather briefcase onto the table and took a seat. "Thank you for your patience. I am Phillip Westbrook, though you probably know that. Sadie, nice to see you again. I remember when you used to come visit your father when he had his law firm. Give him my best, will you?"

Clearly Sadie and I were not in the mood for small talk and did not acknowledge his request either way. We simply sat and watched him with imploring eyes, waiting to be told what my future held. "Right," he said, reading our expressions. He opened his briefcase and took out a folder and yellow legal pad before closing it and placing it beside his chair. "You're probably wondering what is happening. Don't worry. I'll be here every step of the way." Mr. Westbrook folded over the first few pages of the pad which were scribbled in notes, until he came across a clean page. "I have been taking care of Dee Dempsey's legal affairs and, in turn, have become Veronica Dempsey's attorney in this case."

I followed his words, waiting for the triggers: murder, arrest, victim, jail. But none of them came. I glanced at Sadie who tucked away her emotions and became attentive to Mr. Westbrook. I saw her father in her at that moment.

"New evidence has come to light in the case of Dee Dempsey's death which makes it a murder case. Before we can move forward with the case, Veronica Dempsey would like to speak with you," he explained.

Sadie's eyebrows met in confusion as her eyes swept past mine. Before I could ask any questions, Chief Gomes, Jake, and Veronica entered the room. Solemnly, Veronica sat beside her lawyer while Jake stood in front of the door and Chief Gomes stood beside Veronica, his hands across his swollen belly.

Veronica had been crying. Even more so than when we saw her in the waiting room a few hours ago. Though her eyes were puffy and glistening, she looked lighter than before, as if weights had been lifted.

"Veronica Dempsey has agreed to a signed confession in exchange for this meeting," Chief Gomes explained. My jaw might have dropped to the floor if I hadn't been tangled in a web of confusion. "She was in no way coerced or forced to do so."

"My client also understands that she does not have to do this, but in doing so will receive a break in her sentencing," Mr. Westbrook added, for the record.

"Confession?" I asked, surprised. "What—?"

Sadie kicked me from beneath the table. "I advise you not to speak right now," Sadie muttered, channeling her father's court room demeanor.

Heeding her advice, I closed my mouth and looked from Mr. Westbrook to Veronica. I felt a bit put out by Sadie's forwardness, but she put a reassuring hand on my arm beneath the table, and I knew she meant well.

Before anyone else spoke, Mr. Westbrook whispered a question into Veronica's ear and her long brown hair dragged across her shoulders as she shook her head in response. I glanced at Jake, who stood with his Steno pad open, avoiding my gaze that pleaded for information, for reassurance on his part. Sadie squeezed my arm and my eyes returned to the tortured woman in front of me.

"I love my sister," Veronica started. "Her death hurts me in a way only a twin could understand." In a quieter tone she admitted, "It eats away at me like acid." Her face cracked for a moment, letting quick silent tears fall. "The pain is too much." I empathized with her and felt hot tears rush to my eyes that I desperately tried to blink away.

"I told you before that I was the screw-up. She was the good one—the one who took care of Uncle Henry while I was livin' it up on cruise ships." As she spoke, she looked between me and the tissue in her hands. The band of her stainless steel watch made sounds as it constantly clashed with the hard surface of the table.

"Well, I got into some trouble," Veronica admitted, avoiding eye contact. "I wanted out. I wanted to start over, put down roots, especially since Dee was getting married." Tears sprang once again to her eyes and Mr. Westbrook moved the tissue box closer to her with the tip of his pen. She took it with more force than she needed to and blew her nose.

"I worked on cruise ships, right?" she asked with an aggressive gaze. "Well, I formed a bit of a gambling problem. Beginner's luck only lasted so long..." she trailed off. She winced with her next sentence. "I tried to pay it off with illegal transporting—I know how to hide stuff on a cruise ship so it wouldn't be found. It went south. Like everything in my life always does," she admitted. "Instead of owing $10,000, I now owed $50,000."

Veronica's eyes met mine. They pleaded for understanding, for empathy. "I was desperate. I knew Dee had inherited a little more than $25,000 from our uncle." She looked away from me and back down to the tissue in her hands. "I met with her that night."

A fresh batch of tears escaped her eyes and it took a few moments for her to control her emotions in order to speak again. Chief Gomes looked down at Veronica with no emotion on his face. His hands rested on his belt, revealing the strain of the buttons on his uniform shirt that desperately tried to stretch across his belly. Mr. Westbrook scribbled notes on his legal pad. Sadie had a tear fall down her cheek as she watched Veronica unfold.

Shock still prevented me from processing this batch of information. Was this really happening? What was the twist? I looked at Jake who looked back down at his Steno pad when I accidentally caught his gaze. I frowned.

Veronica took a dramatically long deep breath. "Without asking any questions, Dee said yes. She'd give me half of her inheritance. Just like that," Veronica explained, her lips quivering. "'Anything for my sister,' she said. I was so relieved. For once I thought everything was going to work out. I was going to be free from my past..." Veronica trailed off into a sob, but I had lost a sense of empathy for her.

The silent sobbing lasted so long, I thought that our session was over. I shifted nervously in my seat, not wanting to be in that room anymore. I didn't want to hear what came next. Veronica struggled to form words and I could tell Sadie was resisting the urge to ask questions. Her knuckles were white as she gripped the arm of her chair.

"Charli," Veronica pleaded for my attention. "I don't know—I don't understand—" She tripped over her sentence then pugnaciously ripped another tissue from the box in front of her. "I've replayed that night in my head a million times. I can't make sense of it. Why did it have to happen? What could I have done differently? Why do these things always have to happen to me?"

For several moments Veronica let out a heart-wrenching cry. Her shoulders heaved and she wailed into the wad of tissues in her hand. No one put a reassuring hand on her back or broke the soul-crushing sound of loss with questions.

Then, as if on an inaudible cue, her raw voice sliced through her cries. "It had been raining that night," Veronica finally continued. "The entire time I stood in her classroom, I was dripping onto her floor—I wasn't sensible enough to carry an umbrella. That's how I killed her."

Sadie let out a small gasp and I heard Jake busily scratching a pencil on his Steno pad behind me. Mr. Westbrook tapped his pad of paper three times with his pen as he studied his client.

"It was an accident," Veronica said, almost pleading. Her eyes moved around to each person. "It really was. She slipped." Veronica's lips trembled and her hands slipped beneath the table and into her lap. The sound of her watch scrapping against the table was too loud in that room.

"She slipped, backward," Veronica admitted. "She

smacked her head on the corner of her desk." Veronica looked up from her hands and her gaze bore into me. "That sound, Charli, it haunts every moment: it echoes in my dreams and follows me during the day. I will never forget that sound."

Veronica lifted her hands and rested her elbows on the table. She held her forehead in her hands and I watched as a tear fell from her eyes and splashed onto the table. "I panicked," she admitted through the hair that fell in front of her face. Finally, she lifted her head, looking between Jake and Chief Gomes, and continued, "With the people who were hounding me for money... the trouble I was in... I was convinced I'd be pinned for murder. I wasn't thinking!"

I resisted the urge to glance at Jake's response. "So I found a rope in the janitor's closet and..." Veronica struggled to finish her sentence. "She didn't deserve that. It was like I watched myself put the rope around her neck, like I wasn't me—I couldn't stop myself. It felt like the only way. I cried. I couldn't—"

Veronica fought through the tears and continued, "When Lyle called to tell me about Dee, I was in a hotel outside Bloomington." She then turned to the Chief and explained, "Lisle didn't know. He doesn't know any of this. He had nothing to do with it. I came back to Alton Oaks and tried to be of help to him, as some sort of penance. But this secret ate away at me. The people I owed money to knew what I did. He had his monkeys tail me and started blackmailing me— $50,000! I didn't know how to dig myself out—I couldn't; I was stuck. Nowhere to go but down."

The tears had stopped from Veronica and now another emotion seemed to take form. "Then Lyle told me that Dee had left her inheritance to the school—for the arts and to set up some kind of an outdoor education play space. Lyle was mad." Again, Veronica looked up at both Chief Gomes and Jake. "He wasn't mad because he didn't get the money, but because he knew that Principal Newton wouldn't use that money how Dee wanted it spent. When the principal found out about the money Dee had left to the school, she lined up a purchase of test prep books and computer software."

Veronica's face hardened and she stared at the tissue box as if it had pissed her off. "I saw Principal Newton's car in the parking lot that day and pulled in. Charli, you had just left, and you did not look happy. I walked towards the school as Principal Newton was leaving. I wanted to talk to her about Dee's wishes. I needed to make sure Dee got her way in death. She deserved it. I tried to make it right. I walked with Principal Newton to her car. I offered to be an advisor or the program manager of Dee's dream. I knew what Dee would've wanted, but that woman had her mind made up. I pleaded with her. I told her the money was for the kids and that Dee was all about what was best for the kids."

With Veronica obviously getting upset, Chief Gomes moved a step closer when she pounded her fist onto the table. Looking straight at me, she explained, "That woman wouldn't listen to me. She acted as if I was below her and knew nothing about education. Our conversation got heated in the parking lot and she finally admitted that Dee's donation was gonna make up for her students' low test scores. Then I snapped."

Speaking forcefully with her hands now, I saw Jake move closer as her watch banged on the table loudly. "I snapped, Charli. It was bad enough that I killed my own sister, but I wouldn't let her life's work go to waste. I wrapped that seatbelt around her neck, used the headrest as an anchor, and pulled until she stopped moving."

The picture she painted sent shivers down my spine.

"I was going to leave town. I was," she admitted in a quieter tone. "It's what I should've done, but I couldn't escape my own prison."

Veronica turned to Sadie and her features softened. "Thank you for finding that folder. And for asking questions. Raising attention. Maybe I left it on purpose. I just... I'm glad it's over."

Then she turned to me, her hair falling over her shoulders, and said, "And, Charli, I'm sorry you got involved. I truly am."

Slowly she glanced over her shoulder at Chief Gomes and asked, "Is that all you need? I think I'm done now."

"The lead crime scene detective just called about an hour ago," the Chief explained. "They found your fingerprints on the head rest and seatbelt of Ms. Newton's sedan."

Mr. Westbrook put his pen down and rubbed the bridge of his nose where his glasses rested as Chief Gomes read Veronica her Miranda rights, handcuffing her. As Jake opened the door and Chief Gomes guided Veronica out, she turned back and met my gaze with pain in her eyes. "Please," she said, looking between Sadie and me. "Please know that I loved my sister. She was a saint. No matter what happens, please let that be the memory of her that lives on."

Sadie nodded and squeezed my arm. I agreed as well. It was the least I could do for Dee.

CHAPTER TWENTY-FOUR

The news about Veronica covered the town like maple syrup. Citizens would shake their head in disbelief while others would smugly nod and say, "I saw it comin'."

Each day that passed, the story got watered down while news of divorce, new love, and he said/she said-isms buried it. It was still there; it would always be a scar on the town, but now we could get back to the small-town gossip instead of who killed who.

Three months of sweltering summer weather had passed in Alton Oaks without another murder or suicide. Things were finally getting back to normal.

In mid-August, Sadie and I walked down Oak Street together, our skin a few shades darker from the summer sun and weekends on the river. We were attending the opening ceremony of the Dee Dempsey Greenhouse & Outdoor Play Area of the Alton Oaks school district.

Shortly after Veronica was sentenced for voluntary manslaughter, Mr. Westbrook came up to me on behalf of Lyle Woodridge and the superintendent of River Oaks Elementary. "It would be a great honor," read the letter Lyle sent me, "if you supervised this project. It would give me peace of mind knowing someone as passionate as Dee would oversee the development of her wishes."

All summer I worked hand-in-hand with Willa to develop the project and supervise the building and construction. "It will give Veronica peace of mind," Sadie said as I considered the role. "In at least one area of her slightly damaged mind." For some reason Sadie empathized with Veronica and I couldn't understand why.

"Do you regret any of it?" Sadie asked as we cut through the footpath behind the Kratsky house. We could hear the school's band playing a choppy rendition of the school song in the distance.

I was taken aback by her question. Why would I regret any of it? I felt a sense of purpose. "No, not one moment. I'm excited it's finished," I explained as we spilled out into the elementary school's parking lot. Between the gardens surrounding Town Circle and the school's baseball and football fields was an open meadow the school used for overflow parking. It was the perfect place for Dee's project.

As we rounded the corner of Sheridan Avenue and past the baseball field, the greenhouse stood glinting in the late afternoon sun against the backdrop of the Whett River Canal.

A crowd of Alton Oak citizens formed on the field outside the greenhouse. Children of all ages were already playing in the outdoor play space: running in and out of the play cabin, making mud pies, swinging from the tree houses held together by a small ropes course. The architect and landscaper also had formed a small, shallow brook that ran through and eventually emptied into the river. Children were building dams with the rocks, splashing and laughing in the late sun.

"Hello, ladies." I turned to see Rip eating a stalk of corn on the cob wrapped in a napkin and dripping in butter.

"Where have you been all summer?" I asked, almost chastising him.

"And where did you get that?" Sadie asked, putting her hand on her rumbling stomach. When Rip pointed towards Town Circle, Sadie disappeared from my side.

"Well?" I asked, raising an eyebrow.

He reached into his pocket with his free hand and pulled out a business card. Handing it to me, he reported, "Working on my business plan."

Looking down, I read his new business card. "Handyman Extraordinaire?"

He took another bite and wiped the butter and loose kernels off his chin, nodding. "Something your town doesn't have."

Reading off his card, I quoted, "Repairs, Pipes, Drywall, and Dreams. There's nothing broken I can't fix." I looked up at him with a doubtful eyebrow raised. "Really? Broken dreams?"

He smiled. "It got your attention."

I rolled my eyes and handed the card back to him. "Keep it," he said, raising his hand. "You might find someone who needs my skills. Pass it on."

Doubtful, I pocketed the card.

"Crazy summer, huh?" he commented, taking another bite. Part of me hoped Sadie would bring me back something to munch on too.

I didn't respond, but turned and continued walking towards the greenhouse. Rip kept up beside me, munching on his snack.

A makeshift stage had been built by Walter, who weaved through the crowd, picking up garbage and placing it in the bag attached to his belt. Once a ghost that no one paid attention to, now people were stopping to ask him about his day, and offering him samples of the food being sold by the PTA. I watched as he politely declined and continued on his way. Our gaze met briefly and his eyes crinkled in the corner with a smile. I returned it with a small wave.

Jake came through the crowd from the east. He was on duty in his uniform. I waved at him when I caught his eye and motioned for him to come on over. Without a smile or any form of acknowledgement, he turned in another direction and disappeared into the crowd.

"What's wrong with Dudley Do-right?" Rip asked, eating the last bit of his corn and dropping the cob in the nearest trash can.

I rolled my eyes. I couldn't believe those two just couldn't get along. I guess it made sense: local bad boy and the town's deputy. They were as opposite as could be.

"Don't do that," I chastised. "And I don't know." I wondered what was up with Jake. All summer he had been elusive and when I did see him, he avoided me or had somewhere else he needed to be.

"Did you know they have hot dogs, and funnel cakes, and cotton candy for sale? This is better than Founder's Day!" Sadie exclaimed, rushing up to me with a hot dog. Alex wasn't far behind her. "And look who I found spinning some cotton candy!" she exclaimed, pulling on Alex's hand.

Without asking, I dipped my hand into my brother's bag of cotton candy and pulled out a chunk for myself. "Thanks, bro," I said with a full mouth.

Rip pulled out his business card and began talking with Alex as Sadie and I walked closer to the stage. "We might have had a lot of bad things happening in Alton Oaks lately," Sadie mused, "but you can't say good things aren't happening too."

We watched the reflection of the sunset in the panes of the greenhouse as Willa Corden, River Oaks Elementary's new principal, started organizing the beginning of the night's festivities on stage. "You did this," Sadie said, staring at the town's celebration.

"Not me," I argued.

"You played a big part," she commented. Playfully nudging me in the side with her elbow, she took a bite of her hot dog and said, "Face it, Charli. Where would

Alton Oaks be if you never moved back?"

I smiled. The past five months had not been easy, but Alton Oaks did feel more and more like home again.

THE END

ABOUT THE AUTHOR

Megan Rivers is a former world adventurer and life-long writer who graduated from Northern Michigan University with a degree in writing and literature. She recently returned to live in her hometown of Evergreen Park, Illinois, with her spoiled pup Gracie. She teaches outdoor and environmental education. When not writing, she loves to visit thrift stores, bask in the outdoors, get lost in a good book, or cook delectable vegan dishes. Her first book in the Alton Oaks Mystery series was *Murder in Aisle Three.*